THE MIND SIEGE PROJECT

THE MIND SIEGE PROJECT

definetly

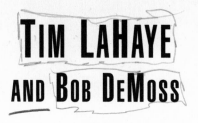

TIM LaHAYE
AND BOB DeMOSS

W PUBLISHING GROUP™

www.wpublishinggroup.com

A Division of Thomas Nelson, Inc.
www.ThomasNelson.com

ISBN 0-8499-4299-3

Printed in the United States of America

03 04 05 PHX 5 4 3 2

For my firstborn son
Robert G. DeMoss III
May this inspire you to carry the torch
—BOB DEMOSS

Prologue

At the edge of the marina, a lone figure sat in his car and checked his watch: 5:53 A.M. He looked up and, with a squint, his dark eyes focused on the activity below.

He noted that six students had already arrived and were busy lugging their luggage aboard the houseboat. He knew a few of them, at least by name.

They, however, would never forget his.

He grabbed his denim backpack from the seat beside him and, with care, retrieved the seven-inch knife buried beneath a change of clothes. He held the blade up to inspect the tip. The sunlight danced along its razor-sharp edge, as if fearful of the cold steel.

A twisted smirk pierced his face. Would they scream? Would they cry for help? Would they be able to stop him?

No. Of that he was sure.

A voice from some deep, neglected space inside his mind interrupted his thoughts. It whispered: *Don't do it! Do you really think you're gonna heal the pain by causing more pain?*

He hesitated.

For a short moment, he shifted his focus from the knife to the early morning sun as it sprayed warm bursts of red color over the surface of the Chesapeake Bay. He spotted a pelican perched on the well-worn pier next to the houseboat, and as he sat in the stillness, he inhaled the steady, warm Atlantic breeze that drifted ashore. Overhead, the clouds that stretched across the sky embraced the dawn like an old friend.

With his left hand he tapped his fingers on the steering wheel. Was there another way?

Could he turn back the clock and stop what he had set in motion? A wave of doubt washed over him. Maybe he could confide in someone. But whom? Not his folks. No way. Then whom?

And if he managed to find someone, would they understand his feelings—or have him arrested and sent to a juvenile detention facility?

The alarm on his wristwatch yanked him back to the present. Six o'clock. A minute more and he'd be late.

His pulse quickened as his eyes darted one last time between the students on the dock and the knife in his right hand. He knew once he stepped on the boat, there would be no turning back.

His mind was made up.

The houseboat would be the place.

This is how he would be remembered.

He hid the dagger at the bottom of his bag, got out of his car, and joined the others at the boat.

Saturday
Fisherman's Wharf, Chesapeake Bay, Maryland

6:02 A.M.

"No way am I going to set foot on that old clunker!"

Heather Barnes set her suitcase on the ground and crossed her slender arms, her eyes fixed on the seventy-five-foot houseboat stretched out before her. "What a relic," she said. Although tethered to the dock, the *Dreamweaver* creaked and groaned in unison with the cadence of the bay waters.

"Just look at it," Heather said to her best friend, Jodi Adams. "It's nothing more than a rusted-out floating tin can, and I don't intend to spend my spring break stranded somewhere out there in that . . . that lousy excuse for a boat."

This was clearly not what either of them had pictured when their social studies teacher, thirty-nine-year-old Rosie Meyer, described the opportunity to spend seven days on a houseboat discussing the issue of tolerance . . . for extra credit. "What better way to grasp the need for tolerance in society," Mrs. Meyer had queried, "than to live in close quarters with people from diverse backgrounds?"

1

TIM LAHAYE & BOB DEMOSS

Rosie had called it "Project Houseboat," and the opportunity was open to all of her honors students, though space was limited. Jodi and Heather had jumped at the chance to participate. Why not? Eight junior class students sailing the Chesapeake Bay with Mrs. Meyer sure beat sitting at home channel surfing. Plus, the brochure's description of two WaveRunners, the twelve-foot sliding board off the back of the boat, and the promise of cliff diving were a huge added bonus.

Jodi and Heather had gotten their parents' permission, raised the activity fee of $425, and counted the days. But at the moment, Heather was ready to jump ship before even setting foot on it.

"It doesn't look so bad to me," Jodi said. "What did you expect, a Carnival Cruise ship? It's got, um, character. Come on, you can do this. It'll be a blast!"

"I can't."

"Sure you can, Heather. You know how hard we worked to earn the money to go on this trip. We've planned it for months. And we're gonna be roommates, right? What could go wrong? Besides, didn't Mrs. Meyer say her husband, what's his name . . ."

"Phil."

"Yeah, he's an ex–Navy Seal or something. He's gotta know boats. I'm pretty sure we wouldn't be taking this one anywhere if there was something wrong with it. Right?" Jodi put her arm around Heather. "Come on, girl. Last one on swabs the deck!"

Heather didn't move. Instead, she tossed Jodi a sideways glance. Jodi couldn't miss the look of apprehension in her eyes.

"You wanna know the truth?" Jodi leaned toward Heather so she wouldn't be overheard. "Okay, I confess. This boat isn't what I had in mind, either. We'll just have to deal with it. But you know what? I'm more nervous about spending a week with people I don't really know anything about. Aren't you?"

"Um, not really." Heather tucked her hair behind her left ear. "Why?"

2

"I mean, what will the other students be like? Don't most of them have social studies together in a different period? Plus, I bet we're the only Christians on board."

Heather raised an eyebrow. "Isn't that the point . . ."

"I know. You don't have to say it. We prayed about taking a stand for Christ at school . . ."

"And, like you said, this is the perfect chance to be a witness," Heather said.

"Guess as long as you're coming with me, I can handle it." With that, Jodi smiled, picked up her suitcase, and started for the boat. She turned her head and said, "Let's go!"

Heather didn't budge.

"Earth to Heather . . . Let's get going or I'll personally push you off the pier into those shark-infested waters," Jodi said.

"There's sharks down there?" Heather reached for the wooden railing.

"You're unbelievable! I'm just kidding."

"Would ya looky here," a voice from behind them said, followed by a hearty catcall. "Two lovely ladies. Going my way? I'm Stan Taylor, but you probably knew that already."

He held out his hand as if it were a prize to possess.

"I'm Heather . . . Heather Barnes." She shook Stan's hand with a giggle. "This is Jodi."

Jodi recognized Stan as a star player on the football team. Half the school called him "Stan da man," and his reputation as a ladies' man appeared to be right on target. Jodi just nodded and offered a forced smile.

"Whoa! Iceberg central." Stan pretended to be hurt. "Guess I'll just board the *Titanic* and save ya a seat." He walked down the boardwalk, then turned back and added, "If they run out of seats, you could sit in my lap, Jodi." With a smirk he flung his bag over his shoulder and boarded the houseboat.

Heather waited until Stan was a safe distance away before she

3

said to Jodi, "I can't believe Stan Taylor is on this trip! He's gotta be the most popular guy at school. Word is he'll probably end up with a full ride at Penn State."

"Yeah, if he doesn't trip over his ego first."

"He was just flirting, Jodi. He *is* kinda cute . . ."

Rosie Meyer stood on the deck of the boat and placed a bull-horn to her lips. A blast of feedback erupted, forcing Jodi and Heather to drop their suitcases and cover their ears.

"Ouch! Guess I won't be needing to use Q-Tips this week," Jodi said to Heather.

Rosie adjusted the volume and tried again. "Ladies, would you like a personal invitation or perhaps a red carpet rolled down the plank before you come aboard?"

Her tone was friendly but direct.

"In case you hadn't noticed, this isn't the Ritz-Carlton and there are no embroidered terry robes hangin' in your closet. However, we'd sure enjoy your company—and let me just add we're waiting on you before we can shove off." Rosie offered them a smile, turned, and began to untie the ropes that secured the houseboat to the dock.

"Guess I'm thankful I watched all of those *Gilligan's Island* reruns as a kid," Heather said.

"How's that?"

"At least I'll know what to do if we get stranded on a deserted island." Heather flashed Jodi a smile.

Jodi grinned. "You're a nut case. Come on. And don't forget I get the top bunk."

Jodi and Heather climbed aboard, made their way around the deck to the forward cabin, and stepped in. They paused to survey the interior. A large, cozy, yet modest living space with windows on two sides greeted them. The inexpensive miniblinds covering the windows were drawn, permitting plenty of sunlight to warm the room. Pale white linoleum flooring extended from the living room to the simple yet fully functional galley.

A Formica-topped table and chair set were positioned in the adjoining dining area. In the corner they noticed a spiral staircase leading to the upper floor. They would soon discover this main cabin area would serve as the general meeting and eating room for the group.

The sound of footsteps racing across the deck caught their attention. Another student, Bruce Arnold, stormed through the door behind them. "Excuse me," he said, out of breath. When they didn't immediately move, he said, "Could you take up a little more room here? I forgot something in my car." He flashed them a grin.

With a wave of their hands, Jodi and Heather let him into the room.

Heather took a seat on the pale green sofa. Jodi glanced around the room and discovered all of the other seats were taken. Her eyes met Stan's long enough for him to transmit the idea that his lap was still available. She blushed.

Jodi wrinkled her nose and managed to mouth the words, "I'd rather stand."

The engine jolted to life and, with a heave, the *Dreamweaver* reluctantly pulled out of its dockside position. Several in the group applauded.

"Let's *ROCK!*" Stan said with a shout, his muscular arms pumping the air above his head.

Jodi took a deep breath and managed to keep her cool as the deck rattled and groaned while the houseboat picked up speed.

6:06 A.M.

"Welcome to Project Houseboat!"

Rosie bounded through the forward doorway. Her short, cropped, chestnut brown hair framed a wide grin. "In all my years of teaching,

I've never had the joy of doing something as exciting and as cutting-edge in education as this."

She clapped her hands together, barely able to contain her enthusiasm. "I'm glad each one of you is here—especially so early on a Saturday morning. Thanks to the board of Huntingdon Valley High School, who gave us the thumbs-up for this unique experiment, we're gonna have the time of our lives—that I promise."

"Mrs. Meyer? Excuse me, but what happened to the boat in the brochure? This tugboat is, well, kinda dumpy," Bruce said. Everyone nodded.

Rosie smiled. "You're right. This isn't the boat we arranged to take. Evidently that unit developed engine trouble. You can imagine, most everything is rented over spring break, so they've given us a discount on this 'classic' vessel," she said. "Hey, I thought retro was cool. Come on, gang. We've got great food, tons of activities, and awesome learning sessions planned."

Rosie walked to the center of the room and continued. "At the same time, I know there may be those who are uncertain about this whole boat thing." She looked in the direction of Heather and offered an encouraging smile. "Not to worry. In a minute I'll introduce you to my husband, who is, trust me, overqualified to run this ship. But first, I'd like to—"

"Mrs. Meyer?" Stan interrupted.

"Yes?" Rosie said. She sighed. She had Stan in third period. If only he'd spend a fraction of the time studying that he invested in bodybuilding and football practice, he wouldn't be falling behind in class. Yet, Rosie could identify with the drive to push his body in competition.

Back in 1980, she had won a silver medal for freestyle swimming at the Summer Olympics. She knew the drill. The endless hours doing timed sprint laps in the pool. The use of weights to strengthen various lower muscle groups. Bicycle riding three days a week to increase leg strength.

To become a world-class athlete, discipline, focus, and commitment must push away all other priorities. On that level, Rosie understood Stan.

"I've got a question. Where's the TV?" Stan asked.

Someone snickered.

"Sorry to disappoint you, but there isn't one," she said.

His face fell.

"Since you brought it up, I might add there are no phones, no computers, no e-mail access, and no way to contact the outside world other than the ship's radio and my cell phone—which probably won't work out on the bay. Now where was I? Oh, I'd like to take a moment—"

Stan cut in. "What, no ESPN for an entire *week?* How am I gonna *live* without *SportsCenter*? Nobody told me I volunteered to be on 'Survivor Island'!"

Rosie shook her head. She knew Stan, as the star offensive guard on the football team, had faced adversaries bigger than his six-foot-four, 250-pound frame without a hint of fear. On several occasions she had watched the opposing team try to blitz Stan's quarterback, but his driving knockdown stopped them cold. *Now, ironically, the prospect of no TV has him sacked*, she thought.

"Cheer up, big guy. I have a hunch you'll be so busy with stuff you've never done before you won't even miss it," Rosie said.

"But—" Stan began to protest.

"Please, let the lady talk," Phil Meyer said with a hand gesture toward Rosie. He spoke the words in a flat, even tone that sounded as much a threat as a promise. He had appeared in the room, almost phantomlike, out of nowhere.

Rosie tucked her hair behind her ear as she admired Phil's tall, slender body. She knew, though average-looking at first glance, he was a finely tuned machine, a by-product of serving twenty years as a member of the elite Navy Seals Special Forces unit. She liked the way his jeans and Windbreaker were loose enough to conceal his

well-toned, muscular physique. His hair, a midnight black without
a hint of gray, was a crew cut, buzzed with angular precision just
the way she preferred it.

"People, I want you to meet my husband, Mr. Meyer," she said.
He waved off the formal title. "Please, call me Phil."

Rosie could see Stan sizing up her man. "So this is Mr. Special
Forces we've all heard about . . . Doesn't look so tough to me."

She watched as Phil and Stan locked eyes.

"Tell ya what," Stan said, his voice self-assured. "Why don't we
start with a little arm wrestling? Or, if you want, we could slide back
a few chairs and go a round right here . . . that is, if you're up to it."
Rosie watched Stan gesture to the area in the middle of the room
as he spoke.

Rosie knew Phil couldn't be bothered with Stan's challenge by
the way he cocked his head. She and Phil had privately shared a
laugh at the countless times he'd been challenged before by
assorted punks and skinheads, each possessing more brawn than
brains. If one of them discovered Phil was an ex-Seal, they'd feel
compelled to challenge him to a fight. Happened all the time—like
some ancient rite of passage. Stan just managed to be more obnox-
ious than most.

Without offering a response, Rosie watched Phil disappear
down the back hallway to navigate the boat.

"He's a man of few words, but he's my sweetheart," Rosie said
with conviction. "By the way, Stan, I think you better not push him.
He can be a bear when he wants to." She gave Stan a wink for
emphasis.

Stan crossed his arms and then puffed out his chest. "I can take
him," he said under his breath.

"Well, let's take a moment to get to know each other better.
Some of you are in the same class, but there are students from three
different periods represented. Let's start with Stan, since he's managed to open his mouth." She gave him a sharp grin. "Just give us

your name and, if you'd like, the reason you decided to be a part of Project Houseboat."

Before Stan could speak, Rosie added, "Keep in mind none of us has had breakfast yet, so keep it brief," then sat cross-legged on the floor.

"Stan Taylor, and I'm here to pick up chicks." He laughed at his own joke. "Hey, now that I broke up with my girlfriend I'm a free man, right? Seriously, I needed the extra credit and figured what cooler way to get it than to go boating . . . with a few babes." He sat back against the wall and gave Jodi a wink.

"I'm Carlos Martinez." He stood up as he spoke. He appeared relaxed and confident, sporting a pair of jeans that fit neatly on his trim frame, along with a green polo shirt that complemented his olive complexion and black hair.

Carlos looked around the room. "When Mrs. Meyer described this as a way to explore the issue of tolerance, it sounded compelling. You may have guessed, I'm Hispanic. I know firsthand what it's like not to fit in. I thought I might learn something new about transcending societal barriers." He returned to his seat and looked to the boy on his left.

"Wow! I'm Bruce Arnold and I need a decoder ring to figure out what Carlos just said." He gave Carlos a friendly elbow and they shared a laugh. Bruce, like Carlos, wore denim jeans, although his were larger to accommodate his husky body, and a Phillies T-shirt. "All I know is I'm interested in the topic and can't wait for breakfast!"

More laughter.

"I empathize with Carlos," Vanessa said. She crossed her long legs, leaned forward, and folded her delicate hands as she spoke. She wore a bright pink turtleneck and black jeans. "I'm Vanessa Johnson, and since I intend on majoring in African-American studies at Temple University, this trip with its emphasis on tolerance seemed too good to pass up. You know, as pre-college-prep and all that." She gave Carlos a quick thumbs-up.

Rosie had to smile. Vanessa always worked hard to sound eloquent. Probably put as much effort into her choice of words as she put into arranging her hair; each strand looked as if it had been assigned a specific spot on Vanessa's head.

"Kat Koffman," said the girl to Vanessa's left. She chewed gum as she spoke. "My mom figured this would be a safer place for me to be than partying every night of spring break." She paused to blow a small bubble. "Of course, the second I left for this trip she took off to the casinos in Atlantic City for the week—maybe longer. I'd say that's a double standard—but hey, with Stan here, maybe there's still hope for our own private party."

Rosie noticed Kat giving Stan a mischievous grin, then, with a pucker, pretending to blow him a soft kiss. His eyes widened with delight.

"Cool," Kat said, nodding her head as if taking a rain check for later that night.

Jodi said to Heather, "Hey, what do they think this is, the *Love Boat*?"

Heather raised an eyebrow.

Rosie had overheard Jodi's comment. She knew Heather must be feeling the same way. Both had signed a True Love Waits pledge card last summer. While Heather had lost her virginity before becoming a Christian, she now shared Jodi's desire to remain sexually pure until marriage. At least that's what the girls had said during an open session on sexual choices earlier in the semester.

The guy in the black T-shirt and black jeans spoke up.

"Justin Moore."

The group waited for him to continue. Nothing.

He crossed his arms and leaned back on his folding chair, a faraway look in his eyes. A moment later, he signaled with his hand as if to say, "Next person."

Rosie noticed that Jodi, who was standing to his side, was caught off guard by Justin's unfriendly tone and stiff body language. *What's bothering him? Why spend money to go on this kind of trip if you're gonna be antisocial?* Rosie wondered.

"Go ahead, Jodi," Rosie said, noticing Jodi's hesitancy.

"I'm Jodi Adams. Um, well, the truth is that I was interested in the tolerance topic especially as it relates to religion."

A quiet, nervous moment passed.

"As a Christian, people make fun of my beliefs all the time. That's probably because of a basic misunderstanding of the Bible." She offered a tentative smile.

"No wonder she's a cold fish," Stan said under his breath, yet loud enough for the others to make out.

Jodi's face reddened. She sat with her mouth slightly open as if to say something. She could have easily defended herself, but didn't want to give Stan the satisfaction of drawing her into a debate.

Heather was quick to bail her out.

"Heather Barnes. Okay, I'm, like, a member of the student council. I'm hoping to be a political science major at Villanova University. Since politics is like one big juggling act, this week on tolerance should be a really cool experience for me."

She pointed to Rosie then added, "Hey, why not let's give Mrs. Meyer a hand for pulling this trip together."

They all clapped.

Everyone except Justin.

His blank expression as he glanced around at the faces of the others concealed what was going on inside his mind.

6:45 A.M.

Rosie stood and signaled to Vanessa to give her a hand. Vanessa hiked up the sleeves on her pink pullover and rose to pass each person a padded leather binder. It contained a yellow legal pad and custom pen. Both items were imprinted with the student's name as well as the inscription "Project Houseboat." As the journals were circulated, Rosie spelled out a brief assignment.

"After you get settled this morning, I'd like for you to take some time alone to write a few paragraphs of what the word *tolerance* means to you. Why is it necessary for society to be tolerant of all viewpoints? How might the world be a better place if we put aside our differences and learned to accept one another? Then provide several examples of people, groups, or organizations that, in your opinion, are intolerant. Be specific. I'll collect those thoughts at lunch. Questions?"

Rosie scanned the faces. "No?" A moment passed. "Yes, Bruce?"

"I'm starving! Do we have to do this right now, or can we eat first?" he asked, patting his stomach. The others laughed in agreement.

"Sure. Let's eat first. Oh, one more thing. Let me remind you, in order to receive full credit for the week, you must maintain a journal of your experiences. I'll be looking for your impressions of this style of learning, and I want you to explore the challenges you personally dealt with. For example, the fear of sleeping on a boat or perhaps the adjustment of rooming with a stranger."

That got their attention. They all looked up from their binders.

"That's right. I realize you may have planned to room with a friend. But in the interest of maximizing this experiment in tolerance, I've paired you with someone who I feel might stretch you this week," Rosie said.

A chorus of displeasure erupted from the students.

Rosie waved off their complaints. She expected this reaction. "My decision is final."

"Hey, does that mean I get to room with a girl?" Stan asked.

"Nice try," Rosie said.

"But Mrs. Meyer," Heather said, "Jodi and I have been planning to share a room for months and—"

"Sorry to disappoint you," Rosie said. "But unless there is some medical reason involved—and I doubt any of you are allergic to one another—I believe this is what's best for our study this week. When we finish in just a minute, please check the roommate arrangement posted on the message board in the galley." She pointed in the direction of a medium-sized, light brown corkboard panel tacked to the side of a cabinet.

"By the way," Rosie added, "Phil and I will be in the captain's quarters on the lower deck. The girls will find their cabins on the upper deck. Guys are on this main level adjacent to us. And your cabins are *not* coed—if you catch my drift. Like it or not, that's the school policy."

Jodi swallowed hard. Whom would she be matched with if not Heather? She could handle Vanessa, if she *had* to. Vanessa seemed levelheaded enough. But what if Mrs. Meyer had placed her with Kat? As far as she could tell, Kat appeared to be, well, different— with a capital *D*. She didn't want to consider that possibility.

Jodi gave Kat the once-over. She couldn't help but notice Kat's tank top was skintight, not to mention that it hovered several inches above Kat's jeans, revealing a pierced navel. Her lipstick, Jodi figured, was something along the line of an eggplant purple. And Kat's ears looked like two well-worn pincushions, with an assortment of earrings, some large, others small, dangling from various parts of her earlobe.

Jodi looked out the window at the rising sun. She whispered a quick prayer for strength. Her thoughts drifted across the colorful horizon. She lingered in thought; the rhythmic slurp of the waves that lapped against the edge of the bow had a mesmerizing effect. It was then that a distant memory surfaced.

She recalled going to summer camp at age thirteen. A dreadful experience, especially for a budding, self-conscious teenager. Several seasoned campers in her cabin took her "snipe hunting." She spent what felt like an eternity standing alone in the woods in her p.j.'s, holding a pillowcase, clucking, waiting for the fictitious snipe to appear.

Meanwhile, the others were back at the cabin eating cake and candy, laughing at the rookie. She was mortified and privately vowed never again to put herself in such a situation.

The only reason she managed to go to Haiti last summer to build houses with Habitat for Humanity was Heather's commitment to be her roommate. Now, at age sixteen, she was forced to share a bedroom with a complete stranger.

She stole another look at Kat.

"One last housekeeping item," Rosie said. "There's no maid service or kitchen staff. Each person has a task, which you'll also find listed on the message board. I've grouped you into teams to help prepare and clean up after our meals—with the exception of breakfast this morning, which Phil should have ready in about ten minutes. See you back in ten."

Jodi was too anxious to move.

Vanessa, who sat closest to the board, was the first to check the listing. She called out, "Hey, Heather, it's you and me, girlfriend. Cabin five."

"Be right there. I'll grab my stuff," Heather said. She gathered her bags and stopped and asked Rosie, "Mrs. Meyer, what's it like to sleep on a boat?"

"The ultimate in comfort, ladies," Bruce said as he rose from his chair. "Once you get over the thought you might drown in your sleep, it's a piece of cake!"

Rosie waved him off. "It's a lot like sleeping on a waterbed," she said.

Heather nodded, but her eyes betrayed her anxiety about sleeping on the boat.

Jodi came alongside of Heather and, with a firm grip, squeezed her arm. Jodi said, "Hang in there." *I'll do the same,* Jodi thought, as she wondered what kind of roommate Kat would be.

Jodi faced Bruce. "Charming. Really, Bruce." Out of the corner of her eye she watched Heather follow Vanessa up the narrow spiral staircase to their quarters on the upper deck.

Kat approached Jodi. She stopped and stood just a few feet away, chewing a piece of gum. Jodi observed a delicate black widow spider tattooed above Kat's right collarbone.

Kat said, "Looks like it's me . . . and the Christian. Ironic, huh? Your God must really have a sense of humor." *She is pleasant enough,* Jodi thought. *No malice intended.*

Jodi offered a courteous smile.

"If it's all the same to you, you can have the top bed," Kat said. "I don't handle heights real well."

Inside, Jodi wrestled with God. How could God match her with someone so unlike herself? And for *seven* days. Sure, she and Heather would get some hang time together, but it wouldn't be the same as talking or laughing and praying together with a friend into the wee hours of the morning. What did she have in common with this bizarre stranger? Was God playing some kind of joke on her?

Yet, in a strange way Kat was right. God *had* answered her prayer—that the Lord use her on this trip to be a witness for Christ— but in *his* own way. He provided a mission field right under Jodi's bunk.

Jodi looked her in the eyes and said, "Works for me."

1:00 P.M.

Lunch was completed. The students had thirty minutes of free time before their first class. Several returned to their room to finish getting settled, while some opted to explore the boat. Stan decided to observe Phil at work in the wheelhouse.

When he entered the upper helm, Phil was maneuvering the port side of the houseboat adjacent to a small, uninhabited island in the middle of the bay. Once in position, with a push of a button Phil activated the windlass, a ratchetlike device in the hull of the ship that lowered the anchor and fifty feet of chain into the deep, bay waters.

Another switch killed the inboard motor, a cantankerous modified Ford engine that refused to stop churning until it had belched a bluish-black diesel cloud.

At the sight of the fumes bellowing out from under the rear deck, Stan was tempted to blurt out, "Holy exhaust, Boatman!" But given the intensity of Phil's movements, he felt it better to just keep a sharp eye on the man as he worked. Several minutes passed.

"Mind if I ask a question?"

"Go ahead," Phil said, preoccupied. To maintain electrical power he fired up the auxiliary generator.

"That black thing with the dials, that's the radio, right?"

Phil nodded.

"Does it work? Looks ancient to me."

"You better hope so. That's our lifeline in case of a sudden storm or an emergency," Phil said.

Stan walked to Phil's side and leaned forward for a better view. "How does it work?"

"It's what they call a VHF radio. Let's see, looks like an old Motorola. Can't quite tell. Nametag's worn off. This knob sets the frequency. To talk to another boat, use channels 68 or 72. The Coast Guard monitors channels 9 and 16, which are reserved for distress signals," Phil said.

"Like calling 911, right?"

"Right. Flip that switch, turn the middle dial to the desired frequency, then hold in the key on the side of the microphone like this to talk."

Stan watched Phil closely.

Phil continued. "Remember, whenever you're finished asking a question, release the key on the microphone for their response."

"How far can it pick stuff up?" Stan asked.

"Depends. Several factors come into play. I'd say given the height and placement of that whip antenna," Phil said as he pointed to the well-worn, white, fiberglass antenna overhead, "probably ten, maybe twelve miles. Then again, if the weather gets really ugly, your range will drop significantly. The waves out here have been known to hit eight to ten feet."

Stan appeared puzzled. "I don't suppose you can pick up any ball games on it then, can ya?"

Phil shot him a bewildered look. "Son, if you'll excuse me, I've got work to do."

He turned his back toward Stan.

"Look, I didn't mean any harm," Stan said, indignant.

Without turning around, Phil asked, "I believe your afternoon session is underway, correct?"

Stan didn't speak. His eyes were fixed on the back of Phil's navy blue skullcap, a formfitting cap pulled just over the top of his ears, as if staring would somehow provoke Phil to face him.

For an instant, those ears reminded him of his father's. Oddly, that was the view Stan remembered most—the backside of his dad's lobes. He saw them whenever his dad watched TV or worked in silence at his desk. And he'd see them when his dad stormed out the front door following another blowup with his mother.

Weird. It had been several years since Stan had made an association between ears and his father. When Stan was twelve, the man Stan had admired ran off with a woman he met on the Internet. A total stranger from cyberspace invaded their home and snatched his dad, leaving his mom to raise two young boys alone and unsupported.

His anger began to flow at the memory, fueled by a deep, pent-up resentment. He focused even more intently on the cap.

The dam snapped.

"I was *just* trying to make a little conversation," Stan said, his voice on edge, rising a notch. "I'm here to tell ya this ain't one of your top-secret missions. We're just a bunch of kids trying to have a good time."

Still no reaction.

It was as if the sight of those earlobes mocked him, beckoning him into a fight—something that, in a more rational moment, would be the farthest thing from his mind.

But he wasn't thinking now.

His adrenaline kicked into autopilot.

Stan took a step closer; he didn't notice how his own pulse began to pound in a wild, frantic beat.

"Let me guess, it was a heavy dose of Agent Orange in some distant jungle that zapped your ability to carry on a basic exchange with a fellow human, huh?" he asked in a mocking tone.

When Phil didn't respond, Stan reached out and seized Phil's left arm. "Hey, I'm *talking* to you, *pal*—"

Before Stan could finish his taunt, Phil whirled around in a seamless, choreographed blur of motion, yanked both of Stan's arms behind his back, and sent his face into a collision with the window jamb.

Stan could feel the unshaven whiskers of Phil's face against his left ear. "If you know what's good for you, don't *ever* do that again," Phil said in a low tone.

Stan swallowed hard. *What kind of psycho was this guy?*

"Listen—and listen good, *boy*. You might be the big man on campus, but you've got a serious problem, see? For the next seven days this boat is *my* campus and you've got no idea who you're messing with."

He whispered his next words for emphasis. "My reflexes have been synchronized to respond with deadly force when confronted by a hostile action. Just like a candy machine—push a certain button and, *presto!* You'll get what you ordered. You just pushed the wrong button, is that clear?"

Stan struggled to break free.

"There's an old saying: 'It's not the size of the dog in the fight, kid. It's the size of the fight in the dog.' And I'm one mean, hungry, mangy dog . . . *got it?*"

For a split second Stan thought Phil might actually take a bite out of his ear. "Yes sir," Stan said through clenched teeth, though his will to fight or to even resist the viselike grip had long since evaporated.

"One more thing. I *never* sleep. I've got eyes in the back of my head. And I've never lost a fight. If you ever try a stunt like that again, who knows, perhaps the Agent Orange that lingers in my system may temporarily overcome me. No telling what I might do to you then," Phil said. A thin, wry smile crossed his face. "Accidents at sea are not uncommon, you know. I trust we're on the same frequency."

He didn't wait for a reply.

"Let's keep this little talk between ourselves. Deal?"

Stan managed a nod. If Phil was trying to scare Stan, he had more than succeeded.

"Better hustle below, *pal.*"

Stan's legs buckled the moment Phil released him.

1:15 P.M.

Rosie called the group together. "Let's get started," she said.

The students were arranged in a semicircle around her; some sat in chairs or on the sofa; others warmed a spot on the floor. Each sat alert and expectant as Rosie laid the groundwork for the week in this preliminary session.

"This morning, when I announced that I would be assigning you a roommate who was a complete stranger, how did you feel?" She paused before continuing. "By the looks some of you gave me, you'd think I was subjecting you to Chinese torture."

They all laughed. Her frankness loosened them up.

"This afternoon, we begin our examination of tolerance. I'd like several of you to report how you feel—now that the initial trauma is over and you've had a few hours to get acquainted," Rosie said.

Heather spoke first. "You really shocked me with this roommate thing. I mean . . . like, Jodi and I are best friends, and we had it all planned out to be roommates. Honestly? Even if she wasn't on the trip, I'm not sure I'd go out of my way to hang with Vanessa . . . nothing against you, Vanessa," she said, looking at her roommate. "The funny thing is, I can already see that, well, even though Vanessa is African-American—which is way out of my personal experience— she's cool. Oh, and I also learned her dad's a big-time Philly lawyer."

"I didn't say he was in the 'big time,'" Vanessa said in mock objection to the proceedings.

"True. But he's done some work for Jesse Jackson and other high-profile civil-rights cases that made the *Philadelphia Inquirer*. I'd call that *big time*," Heather said. "Anyway, she's a sharp cookie. We'll do great."

"Vanessa?" Rosie asked, looking for her view.

"I'd agree. At first glance, I took Heather for a—you know, the typical ditsy blonde without a serious thought in her head. But I was wrong. She's smart and she asks a lot of good questions. Okay, she may not hang loose like one of the sisters, but this girl strikes me as pretty open-minded and easygoing," Vanessa said.

"Anyone else?"

Jodi bit her tongue. *It's easy for Heather to get along with Vanessa—she, after all, isn't some kind of freaked-out party animal like Kat,* she thought. As if being forced to room with Kat wasn't enough to handle, Kat, she learned while they got settled, was fascinated with the Wicca witchcraft movement. Even brought several books on the subject with her. What could she say? *I'm so happy to be rooming with a witch wannabe?*

At the moment, Jodi felt God was asking too much of her. Didn't he know how much she needed Heather for support? She shifted in her chair and began to examine her long, blond hair for split ends.

Sitting beside her, Kat chewed a piece of gum a little bit too aggressively. "I learned Jodi here won the Pennsylvania statewide award in debate for our school. Not bad for a kid who was home-schooled most of her life. She probably spends as much time studyin' as I spend party hoppin'." She blew a bubble.

Jodi blushed at the mention.

Bruce raised his hand. "Allow me to speak for us. I've discovered that Justin here," Bruce pointed to his roommate, who remained quiet, "has perfected the fine art of silence. Pretty much listens to his Walkman while he does these geeky Ninja moves."

Bruce stood for a quick demonstration.

"I think he thinks he's a kung fu master or something," Bruce said. He sat back down after he finished the role-playing. "Anyway, I believe we'll get along just *gro-o-vy*," he said with his best Austin Powers accent.

"Quite nice," Justin said of Bruce's demonstration.

"Wow . . . the mute speaks at last!" Bruce said, playfully.

Justin gave him a blank look.

Rosie thanked them for sharing. "When we get past the stereo-types we have of other people, we become open to understanding and accepting our differences."

Vanessa and Carlos, who sat next to each other on the sofa, nod-ded in agreement.

"You see, part of learning is 'unlearning.' In other words, we must not be afraid to discard outdated ideas or typecasting of people, which, I admit, sometimes run deep in our personal belief systems," Rosie said. "What's more, sometimes it takes courage to uproot those out-of-date beliefs."

"Did you say, '*unlearning*'?" Heather asked. "Just want to make sure I heard you correctly."

"Yes. And here's a good example," Rosie said. "I was raised in the Catholic religion. Every Sunday, my parents required me to go to Mass. Saturday morning it was my obligation to go to CCD—which is the equivalent of Catholic boot camp. And many Friday nights the Catholic Youth Organization had an activity that I had no choice but to attend."

Carlos looked startled. "Sounds like you spent all week at church."

"It sure felt that way. By the time I was your age, I knew all of the saints by name, and I knew what request, if rubbed the right way, they'd answer for me," Rosie said with a roll of her eyes.

This bit of personal history was news to the students. As a rule teachers didn't discuss matters of religion with students at school and, as such, they knew little of her views on church. However, the houseboat, which blended off-campus vacation time with academics, was an educational hybrid of sorts. Rosie seemed intent on bending the regulations a bit.

"Don't worry, I'll spare you the angry nun stories," Rosie said with a laugh.

Stan tiptoed into the gathering room. If he had hoped to slip in unnoticed, he failed miserably. Jodi thought he appeared about as graceful as a ballerina with an ingrown toenail.

"Glad you decided to join us, Stan," Rosie said.

"Sorry I'm late. Me and Captain Ahab were just having afternoon tea together," Stan said with a point toward the upper deck, then plopped down in the remaining chair.

"I'll let it slide this time, Stan, but don't be late again. Remember, if you want the extra credit, you need to be on time for all our sessions. Fortunately, we've just started. So, as a Catholic," she said, examining Stan as she spoke, "I was taught that truth was absolute and that somehow God had something to do with the dispensing of truth. My priest said the Bible and the pope were the Church's ultimate source for all truth."

She paused. "Stan, are you feeling okay? You look drained and a little pale."

"Just a touch of queasiness. Maybe it's motion sickness," he said, painfully aware everyone was beginning to observe his discomfort. "Don't worry about me. I can take care of myself."

"Okay, but let me know if you need some water," she said.

Stan nodded and opened his binder, but looked as if he might black out.

Rosie continued. "In fact, I was taught that morality, what we consider to be right and wrong, flows from the Bible. Now that I'm older, I've discovered how narrow-minded the notion of absolute truth really is, especially since we now know the Bible is a collection of unsubstantiated claims, mixed together with Near-Eastern legends. It took me four years of college to detox, to 'unlearn' what I had accepted as a young person."

Jodi sat still, deep in thought. She was troubled by this hostile line of reasoning. Why did Mrs. Meyer feel the need to start their week with a discussion attacking absolute truth? What did *that* have to do with tolerance, anyway? And why begin a lesson on being tolerant by saying you don't tolerate something?

Her head swirled with the irony. The debater in her was aroused to defend her Christian convictions, which were being bashed. But she managed to hold her tongue. She'd wait for the right moment to speak.

"I'm curious. What brought about the change in your thinking?" Vanessa asked.

"A willingness to be open-minded and a desire to bring people together, not divide them. I came to see that religion divides people into groups," Rosie said. She leaned forward and retied the lace on her left sneaker.

Rosie continued. "For example, at the center of the Buddhist religion are the Four Noble Truths. They teach that we should give up all desire and stop craving that which is transient in this life. By

practicing wisdom, good behavior, and meditation, Buddhists believe we can eliminate suffering. Eventually the faithful will reach
a state of consciousness called 'Nirvana'—and I'm not talking about
the nineties grunge rock band!"

That got a laugh.

"Rats. I always liked their music," Kat said.

Rosie didn't miss a beat. "Many Chinese revere and follow the
teachings of Confucius. And Muslims all over the world seek to
please Allah by having their good deeds outweigh their bad ones.
Some Muslims even believe that to fight against the enemies of
Allah and to die in the effort is to gain instant access to heaven."

"We read something about that in history," Bruce said. "What
I don't get is how they could convince people to believe that com-
mitting suicide actually *got* you into heaven. I mean really. Where's
the proof? What if they're wrong? Not only are you dead, but you're
in hell—or wherever. Not my idea of a bargain."

"Good point," Rosie said, affirming his participation. She continued. "Then there's the atheist who doesn't believe God or
heaven exists at all. Of course, I was raised to think the Catholic
Church was your ticket to heaven, that is, if you did enough good—
and gave them your money."

Vanessa nodded. "Like those preachers on TV who promise
miracles *if* you send them money. They're a bunch of phonies."

"So who's right? Can you see the problem we have when one
religion claims it holds the *only* way to God or that they are the sole
keepers of truth?" Rosie asked.

No one spoke.

After a moment, Rosie added, "Don't be afraid to say what you
think. All opinions are welcomed."

Her smile was warm and inviting. "In fact, having read the papers
you submitted earlier today, let me ask Vanessa to describe her experience with an organization she felt was intolerant. Vanessa?"

"Well, I remember being invited to a Young Life meeting once after school. What bothered me was how the speaker claimed Jesus was the *only* way to God. When I confronted him about it after the meeting, he explained that according to the Bible, all other attempts to get to God are futile. Can you believe the nerve? So Gandhi goes to hell, then? That's so narrow-minded."

She paused. "That, to me, is the ultimate in intolerance. What about all of the other ways to get to God?"

Jodi raised her hand then said, "Vanessa, that's a total mis-characterization of Young Life. I know the leader. He's a fun, easy-going guy. No way do I believe he'd be so rude, or so . . . so tactless for that matter."

"I'm just telling you what I heard," Vanessa said, then looked away.

Rosie picked up on Vanessa's thought. "Of course, let's not just pick on Christianity. If we're honest, *all* of the world religions tend to be like exclusive clubs. It's, shall we say, their way or the highway."

Bruce cut in. "You can say that again. I remember two guys who came to our front door one Saturday morning. They wore white shirts, black pants, and ties. Must have been poor since they rode bicycles," he said with a chuckle. "The taller guy did most of the talking. Boy, were they persistent. He gave me a newspaper, something about a watchtower."

"I've seen those guys riding around the neighborhood too," Kat said. "When they came to our house, I opened the door and pre-tended to cast a spell on them."

Bruce chuckled. "Frankly, I was in the middle of a video game, so as the guy rambled on and on about the watchtower, I joked, 'My watch is just fine.' They didn't laugh. Talk about uptightsville. All they wanted to do was argue about stuff I didn't understand. What's with that?"

Rosie said, "Well, when people think they're the sole keepers of truth, they tend to be like the stiff-necked, backwoods-preacher type, or they're arrogant like those who follow the Jerry Falwell brand of pious fundamentalism. My problem is that this crusader mentality fuels intolerance—even hatred in society. Can you think of an example from current events?"

"Yeah. I remember that news story about those whacked-out guys who dragged a man to death behind their pickup truck just because he was gay," Carlos said. "I think they were Christians, or Nazis . . . something like that. Anyway, I'm just saying when you believe you've got the truth on your side and someone comes along who is different from you, look what happens."

"But wait a minute," Stan said. "What I don't understand is why the media made such a big deal out of that story—you know, they called it a hate crime just because the guy who was killed was gay. But remember the Columbine High School shooting?"

"Who could forget it?" Rosie said, glad to see Stan was feeling well enough to participate.

"Well, our coach brought in a magazine article that said one of the two shooters . . . what were their names?"

"Eric Harris and Dylan Klebold," Heather said.

"Yeah, one of those guys was gay. Maybe both. Who knows? Maybe they were gay lovers. Did you know that?"

Rosie appeared puzzled. "What's your point, Stan?"

"Nobody in the media called *that* a hate crime, did they? I might not be the brightest kid on the block—I'll admit that. But when the killer or killers are gay, it seems like the news media has a different standard."

Carlos shot back, "What's their sexual preference got to do with *anything*, Stan?"

"Just that if you're a queer . . . excuse me, a fag . . . whatever the right term is . . . you get special treatment."

"I can't believe you're saying that with a straight face," Carlos said.

Jodi thought Carlos's anger with his roommate was about to boil over into a fistfight.

Rosie stepped in the middle of their spat, like a referee at a wrestling match. "All right, let's all calm down. While it may be true that the press sometimes provides uneven treatment of various news stories—"

"You can say that again," Stan said dryly.

"Our goal is to learn how to be more understanding of our differences. And that begins with the choice of words we use. I'm not sure, Stan, that you selected the most conciliatory language when referring to the homosexual community."

Stan crossed his arms; his posture remained defensive.

"I think this exchange underscores our need to grow in our tolerance of diversity—that is, if humanity is to finally come of age," Rosie said. She shut her binder with a snap.

"Okay, everybody," Rosie said. "Let's take a break. You've got free time until dinner, which we'll have on that island at 6:30," she said as she pointed off the left side of the boat. "That's Hog's Head Island. Once we're anchored, see Phil if you'd like to make use of the WaveRunners."

After class was dismissed, Stan avoided eye contact with Carlos as he and Kat left for their rooms. Jodi and Heather lingered to talk, while Bruce, Vanessa, and Carlos headed over to examine the Wave-Runners parked on the rear deck of the boat.

Rosie stopped Justin before he stepped into the hallway.

"Hey, Justin. I wanted to let you know how glad I am you're here," she said with conviction. "I couldn't help but notice you were the only one who really didn't participate. I've read your papers in class and know what you're capable of. Please feel free to join in the discussion at any time. We're all in the same boat, as it were, right?"

Justin avoided direct eye contact with her. "Uh, yeah. Thanks."

With that, Justin retreated to his bunk.

Rosie lingered in the hall, tilting her head as if trying to pin-point the source of her anxiousness about Justin.

She'd ask Phil to keep an eye on him.

7:23 P.M.

The evening sun was low on the horizon. Its golden rays provided little warmth for the students who were snuggled around the open firepit on Hog's Head Island, where Phil Meyer had prepared a cookout of roasted chicken. The sound of the houseboat, which rocked gently in place about thirty yards offshore where it was anchored, could be heard as they licked their fingers for the last time.

"That was the best chicken I've ever had," Stan said to Phil. Several others echoed his sentiment. Phil looked up from his plate with a nod.

Earlier that evening, Phil had shuttled the group to the island in a dinghy that was towed behind the houseboat as a safety pre-caution. As they traveled the short distance to shore in the Starcraft, a five-passenger, fifteen-horsepower boat, Phil had explained the heavily wooded island was uninhabited, though at one time wild pigs had roamed there. According to legend, sailors gave Hog's Head its name when they saw wild pigs peering back at them through the underbrush.

As the last of the paper plates were tossed on the fire, Rosie decided an icebreaker would be good to further loosen up the group. Besides, the students needed to unwind after a long first day. She had just the ticket.

Rosie stood to announce her idea beside the warmth of the fire, which crackled, snapped, and popped as she spoke.

"I'd like each of you to share one thing strange, funny, or odd about yourself that the others wouldn't know," she said, adding, "I'll start."

"How fun!" Heather said.

Bruce laughed, "Yeah, as long as nobody confesses to once being an ax murderer!" He made a chopping motion with his right arm pretending to decapitate Justin, who sat next to him.

The girls squirmed at the joke.

Heather blurted out, "How do you do that, Bruce?"

"Do what?"

"Always manage a joke at the wrong time?"

"It's a fine art, I confess." He smirked.

"If I may continue?" Rosie said pretending to be put out. "I was living in Philly; this would have been 1979. I was a seventeen-year-old seeking some independence, so I figured a little therapy retail shopping in New York City was in order. What better place than Fifth Avenue in the Big Apple, right, ladies?"

They nodded in unison.

"At the end of the day, I put my bags in the car and decided to take a jog through Central Park. Back then I always carried my running gear with me, so I changed at a local service station. When I finished my run, I noticed what looked like a sea of humanity lining one of the streets. Of course, I had to check it out."

"Probably a parade of ax murderers . . ."

"*BRUCE!*" the girls yelled in unison.

"Actually, it *was* a parade," Rosie said. "I pushed my way through the crowd to the edge of the street just as, get this—the pope-mobile was making its way through the city. Everybody was waving and clapping and whooping it up."

"For the pope?" Stan asked.

"You'd be amazed how popular Pope John Paul II is, Stan. Anyway, the pontiff was waving back to the adoring faithful. Just for the fun of it, I reached out my hand as he passed. You'll never guess what he did."

"Slipped ya ten bucks?" Bruce quipped.

"He gave me a holy high-five!"

"No way! How cool is that?" Bruce said, impressed.

Rosie smiled. "I haven't washed my right hand since."

They all laughed.

After a moment, Kat spoke up. "I can't say my unusual secret is anything like that. Promise you won't laugh? For what it's worth, I play the accordion and kazoo at the same time."

Her confession took Vanessa, who was just taking a sip from her Diet Coke, completely off guard. She snorted, sneezed, and sprayed the ground in front of her with a stream of soda.

"And don't ask for a demonstration," Kat managed to say above the laughter.

Over the next several minutes they discovered Vanessa was a closet Ricky Martin fan, Carlos had played the Cowardly Lion in *The Wizard of Oz*, Bruce was a self-confessed addict of the Weather Channel, and Justin would occasionally sleepwalk. That brought a holler, especially with them sleeping on a houseboat all week.

But it was Stan who sent the group rolling on the ground, gasping for air when he confessed that he, Stan da man, loved watching *I Love Lucy* reruns on Nickelodeon.

"Yo, *LUCY*," he said in his best Ricky Ricardo voice, "you've got some 'splaining to do!"

Another wave of laugher.

"What about you, Jodi and Heather?" Stan asked. "Let me guess, you're both secretly in love with me? HA!"

"In your dreams," Jodi said, returning a mock laugh.

She admitted that ever since she was a child, whenever she had cereal for breakfast, she'd pour milk in the bowl, then wait. And wait. She'd wait for the cereal to get completely soggy before taking the first bite.

Heather confessed she loved to eat buttered popcorn with a spoon from a tall glass—*after* she poured whole milk on it.

Even Justin managed to gag over that.

The evening sky darkened and the laughter, like the fire, began to die down. Rosie shifted gears.

"You guys are crazy! I haven't had this much fun in years. But before we wrap things up tonight, let's go around one more time. I'd like for you to consider sharing something more serious that the others wouldn't know. Get only as personal as you feel comfortable. This isn't, by the way, truth or dare."

Heather looked at Bruce. "And none of that ax murderer stuff."

He gave her a sheepish grin.

"I'll start," Rosie offered. "My father was a strict and devout Catholic. He was also an alcoholic. At times, he'd get so drunk he'd rant and rave in the house . . . even throw stuff. My brothers and I would hide under the bed to avoid being hit by him or by something he threw."

She continued, her eyes locked on the fire, almost as if caught in the hypnotic trance of a cobra.

"I'll never forget the time he was so intoxicated, we found him lying outside on the front lawn the next morning, stripped naked. We had to cover him up and drag him back into the house. To say it was a difficult time in my life would be an understatement."

By now, Rosie noticed that the students were feeling a greater sense of togetherness. She was pleased as their responses came in quick, respectful tones, one right after another without any extraneous comments.

"I'm afraid of heights," Kat said. "You know, scared stiff of tall buildings and places like that. I have this recurring nightmare where I'm falling and there's no way to prevent me from hitting the bottom."

The fire crackled as Bruce, sitting next to Kat, considered what to share. "I don't want to die before I've had the chance to do something meaningful in my life," he said. "That's why I've been reading books and magazines on becoming a paramedic."

Jodi poked the fire with a long, bony stick as she began. "You might think this is no biggie. I was a very young kid when I learned my blood type was AB-negative. They said it's very rare, which means if I were, like, involved in an accident and needed blood, well . . ." Her voice trailed off. "That scares me much more than facing an opponent in a hot debate."

Stan's eyes focused on an ember in the firepit as Jodi finished. As he hesitated, Rosie sensed that Jodi's comment sparked an emotion or perhaps a memory in Stan.

"Last summer I needed a little extra cash, so I took a job digging graves at the cemetery near my house. The pay was great, but digging graves every day, ya know, the thought crosses your mind, one day this is how it ends . . . or does it?"

He looked up in the direction of Jodi for an instant. "I've always wondered what happens to me after I die," he said then looked away. "You wouldn't think that a guy as popular as me would ever have those thoughts. Some nights I can't sleep because of it."

Bruce tossed a twig into the fire. "Yeah, I can see how you'd think that. Didn't you have a younger brother who died?"

Stan stiffened. "That ain't got nothing to do with it."

Bruce held up his hands as if in self-defense. "Sorry, just figured it might."

During the next few quiet moments, Carlos revealed he had a sister in college who was a practicing lesbian—which accentuated his interest in the tolerance issue.

Heather's dad, as far as she could recall, had never told her that he loved her.

Vanessa remained silent.

The only sound came from the crackle of the fire and the shrill chirping of the crickets, which competed with the steady cadence of the bay water rolling against the sandy beach.

It was then that Justin spoke, his voice just above a whisper.

"Both of my parents were killed as missionaries in Pakistan. I was in the room when it happened . . . I saw everything. The way they demanded my parents lay facedown on the floor. The way they put the gun first to the back of my mom's head . . . said, 'Curse God or die.'"

He cleared his throat before continuing.

"She said no . . . The gunman shot her right there."

Another pause.

"My father was next. They gave him the chance to live if he'd renounce his God. I remember the way he looked at me through his tears. When the gunmen weren't looking, he mouthed the words, 'I love you' across the room. After they shot him, the murderers left. Guess they didn't know I was hiding under the bed."

He hesitated, his body gently rocking back and forth. He ran his right hand through his hair, pushing the bangs out of his moist eyes.

"I was four or maybe five. Since then, I've learned that militant Islamic forces had instituted an 'antiblasphemy' law. It gives the death penalty for showing allegiance to anybody but the prophet Mohammed. I'm pretty sure they still enforce that provision of the law."

Rosie and the students hung on to every word.

Justin sighed. "When the Pakistani government found me wandering around the streets, they placed me in an orphanage before they released me to my first set of foster parents in the United States. We really didn't get along. A few months ago I was placed with a new set of foster parents . . . They're all right, as parents go."

He looked upward toward the crescent moon hanging low in the sky, then to Rosie.

"I've had a lot of pain in my life. More pain than anybody should ever have to be put through. Why God would allow my parents— who were just trying to do his work—to be murdered, ya know? I still have a reoccurring nightmare about that . . . that night." He suppressed a sob that began to work its way up through his chest.

"I'd rather not say anything more about my past."

He drew his legs up to his chest as if lost in his memories.

It was several minutes before anyone spoke.

Phil stepped toward the now-dying fire, placed another log on the embers, and then confided that he, too, had frequent nightmares. His stemmed from the flashbacks to his days as a Navy Seal. Many of those memories, try as he may, he was unable to forget. He never went anywhere without his 9 mm pistol—just in case.

Bruce said, "Did you ever kill anyone?"

Phil looked him in the eye, "No one who didn't deserve to die."

A new flame licked the fresh wood, casting its glow on the tired faces. Somewhere across the bay a foghorn from a passing ship boomed.

Talked out and emotionally drained, they voted to spend the night under the stars in their sleeping bags—that is, after dessert.

"Who wants to make s'mores?" Rosie asked, holding a supply of marshmallows, graham crackers, and chocolate bars.

11:58 P.M.

He lay awake inside his olive green sleeping bag on the outskirts of the campfire, using his backpack as his pillow. The back of his head rested against the flap, concealing his razor-sharp knife. His dark eyes searched the sky for the moon, which, at present, was concealed by a heavy blanket of clouds.

He was completely motionless—and yet a restlessness stirred within his spirit. With care, he slipped his left arm out of the sleeping bag and checked his watch: almost midnight. He knew the time to act was fast approaching. He had waited a long time for the conversations around him to finally give way to sleep. It was finally quiet. If not tonight, when?

And yet, the island wasn't part of his original plan. The boat had been his first choice. Lying out in the open—especially within view of Phil—presented a set of new risks. Once somebody screamed, well, he'd be stopped before the doorway to death was fully opened. He hesitated in order to rethink the next step.

As he lingered in thought, his mind drifted back to the voices of the girls as they snuggled around the fire after dessert. He recalled how excited they were to be sleeping outdoors—something they hadn't done in years.

If I carry out my plan tonight, they'll have more than their fill of excitement, he thought.

He had to suppress a laugh at their fear of the thick, black woods that covered most of the island. Someone had asked whether there were still wild pigs. Would they be ambushed in their sleep? Do wild pigs have sharp teeth or tusks—or both? What about rabies? What was that sound? Could there be headhunters on the island too? There usually *were* headhunters wherever there were wild pigs, someone else had asserted.

From time to time a sudden blast from a flashlight would pierce the intense darkness as one of the girls aimed the light in the direction of the murky woods. It didn't take long for the girls to scare themselves silly with exaggerated ideas of the legendary wild boars on Hog's Head Island. Some of the guys weren't much better.

What a bunch of sissies, he thought. Funny how the fear of the unknown can play tricks on the mind. Even the shadows take on a sinister personality if you let them.

The talking had stopped about an hour ago. He assumed that the other students, Mrs. Meyer, and Phil had finally fallen asleep. But were they? Was anyone, like him, still staring at the night sky? What about Phil? Did he actually carry his gun all of the time? Did he have it with him tonight? Was Mr. Navy Seal a light sleeper?

He strained as he listened for any signs of life. Nothing. Just the crickets marking time, the sound of the bay waters washing the beach, and the snoring from several exhausted teens.

With a steady, slow movement to minimize the noise, he

unzipped his sleeping bag and, just as carefully, sat upright for a better view of the campsite. He squinted. The inky black darkness was too thick to see much of anything.

He didn't want to risk using his flashlight to assess the situation. His plan would work only if he met no resistance. If only the moon would peek through the clouds, maybe he'd be able to determine whether or not everyone was sleeping.

After what seemed like an eternity, the cloud cover permitted the moon to step out of the shadows for a brief appearance. It cast a faint, bluish white reflection across the island. As the earth was bathed in this dim moonlight, his eyes darted from sleeping bag to sleeping bag before focusing on the spot where Mrs. Meyer and Phil were stretched out.

Were they asleep?

He thought he saw a pair of eyes returning his gaze. It was so difficult to know. He squinted again, more intensely this time.

Phil. He was awake. There could be no doubt about it. Now what?

Could Phil read his mind? Did Phil know what he was up to? Probably not. But to make sure, he pretended to stretch, then yawned and laid back down.

He'd just have to wait for another time.

Maybe tomorrow once they were back on the houseboat.

Then again, maybe later tonight.

Sunday

10:27 A.M.

Rosie, Phil, and the students reboarded the boat after sleeping on the island. The vessel was sailing eastward toward a point in the middle of the bay's 195-mile tributary. The water was relatively calm, the sky bright and clear, although a cloud formation in the distance hinted at a possible midday shower.

A storm of a different kind was brewing in the galley.

"I think it's a bunch of baloney," Stan said to Carlos.

The two roommates were assigned to cleaning up after breakfast. Stan played the gofer. He moved slower than usual; his arms were sore from a restless sleep—thanks to the hard ground. He fetched the used dishes, glasses, and silverware from the table. Carlos washed them by hand in the small, stainless steel kitchen sink.

"What's baloney?" Carlos asked.

Stan stopped his collection and looked in the direction of Carlos. "All that talk yesterday afternoon about celebrating diversity. Especially when it comes to sex. When a guy and a girl get it on, I'm down with that. But two guys? Two girls? No way. It's just not—*natural*."

Carlos returned Stan's look. He set a plate down with a thunk.

"What's your problem, Stan? What does somebody's private sexual choice have to do with you? It's none of your business. Who are you to say what's right or wrong, anyway?" Carlos said.

"What about bisexuals? Let me guess. You think their behavior's okay too. Am I right?" Stan asked.

"It's their decision."

"And transvestites?"

"Again, their choice. What's that got to do with you?"

Stan delivered the last of the dirty tableware, grabbed a moist towel, and quickly wiped the tabletop.

"I'll tell you how. I'd sure hate to get married one day, only to find out later that my wife *used* to be a guy—"

"As if that would ever happen." Carlos shook his head in disbelief. He threw Stan a dishtowel to help him dry off the plates.

"It has! I heard a lady on a radio talk show asking for advice because she got married and, about a year into the marriage, her husband wanted to have children. One tiny problem. *She* was a *he* who had a sex change and never told her husband that she—or *it*—married about that little detail. You're telling me that's not a problem?"

Carlos dried another dish. He didn't answer at first.

"What are you saying, Stan? That gays like my sister are some kind of biological error? Freaks of nature? What?"

"How else do you explain it? I don't know how they got whacked in the head, but that's what they are. Hey, I'm sorry about your sister being a lesbo. But all of this talk about alternative lifestyles—whether you want to admit it or not—is just a cover for the fact that homosexuals are, well, they're like carrier pigeons for the AIDS virus."

"You know what? You suffer from homophobia," Carlos said, then turned his back on Stan.

"And another thing," Stan said, pretending not to hear the accusation, "one day when I'm making a lot of money in pro football, my income taxes are gonna be higher because of the gays and lesbos."

Carlos almost dropped the glass he was holding. "Now I know *you're* the one who's a few fries short of a Happy Meal!"

"I'm serious. It's a fact. I read about this, um, somewhere. Look, where do you think the government gets all of that cash from to find a cure for AIDS? The taxpayer. That's you and me, *pal*," Stan said, jabbing his finger into the side of Carlos. "If your people—"

"My people?"

"The ones you're defending—if they behaved the way God originally intended, we wouldn't be wasting *billions* of dollars treating a deadly disease that is 100 percent avoidable—"

"So now you're bringing God into this? I didn't know you were a right-wing bonehead."

"I'm *not*—"

"But you just said 'God intended'—so you must believe in God."

"I don't know about all that. Besides, you're confusing the issue—"

"Stan, the issue is we just have *different* views about sex. In life, there isn't a rule book. All we can do is learn to respect each other's opinion. 'Live and let live,' remember? Isn't that what this week is all about?"

Stan dried the last plate, placed it on the stack, and then asked, "So you're gay, right?"

"What if I were?"

Stan took a step backward, rolled up his dishtowel into a whip, and pretended to defend himself. "I can't believe I'm rooming with a gaybo."

Carlos waved him off. "Hey, I'm as straight as they come. But like they said in health class, sex is nothing more than a biological function. When people get the urge to merge, you know, they should, like, be free with sex. It's up to them to decide if they feel ready for it. However they want to express themselves is cool with me."

"I still don't get why *I* should be made to pay for the consequences of another person's risky choices. People with HIV should be quarantined."

"And you think sleeping with different cheerleaders isn't risky? The talk around school is you're pretty free with the ladies."

"That's different."

"Oh, now it's Mr. Double Standard. Stan, think about it. You're taking plenty of risks too—like getting a girl pregnant and needing an abortion. You could pick up an STD from them and pass it along to another person and you wouldn't necessarily even know it—like the herpes virus. I just don't think you're in a position to preach."

Stan started to respond. But before he could speak, Rosie stepped into the gathering room and called the students together for their morning session.

11:01 A.M.

"Okay, folks. Don't get too cozy," Rosie Meyer said to the students as they jostled for a comfortable sitting position. "I realize there may be those in our group who traditionally attend religious services on the weekend."

She glanced around the room. Several nodded.

"As evidence that we can learn to engage in mutual respect and tolerance of our divergent views, I'll dismiss you in a minute to find a quiet spot somewhere on the boat where you'll have until noon for personal reflection. Our world is so full of noise it crowds out reflection, which, in turn, makes it difficult for us to learn from silence."

Her voice had a dreamy, light quality about it.

"You may also use this time to catch up with your journal. Whether you chose to commune with the spirit of nature, or with your God—whoever she may be—please focus on your inner self *quietly*. That means no talking and no singing. Each person is to be alone, understood?"

Rosie eyed Kat, who was leaning her back against Stan's legs. "This is not a group project. Questions?"

"Is my bed okay? I do my best reflecting on my pillow in the horizontal position—with my eyes closed," Stan said with a laugh.

"I don't think so. There will be time for that later, Stan," she said.

"What if you don't believe in God and you don't go to church?" Vanessa asked.

"Then let the undefiled elements of the beauty that surrounds us unlock the doorway to personal peace and tranquillity for you," Rosie said pleasantly. "We can all benefit from a little seclusion and personal meditation. All right, I'll see you for lunch in one hour."

Nobody moved. Rosie noticed all eyes were on her.

"Hey, Mrs. Meyer?" Vanessa asked. "Did ya bring your medal?"

"Yeah," Carlos said, "can we *finally* see it?"

Rosie had an idea this was coming. "Only because I'm such a nice teacher . . . Yes, I happen to have it with me."

Several cheered as Rosie reached for her purse and withdrew her gleaming Olympic silver medallion.

"How cool!" Carlos said, staring in awe as Rosie held it up.

"Wow! It's so, well, small . . . I mean compared to what it looks like on TV," Stan said. "Can we touch it?"

"Sure, just be careful . . ." Rosie handed it to Stan first. "It's the only one I'll ever get in this lifetime," she said.

"So what did it feel like when they placed it on you?" Jodi asked.

"Let's see. You could say I was on a natural high, but even that wouldn't be the half of it," Rosie said as the medal was passed around the room. "I was crying, I was happy, I was breathless all at the same time. Partly because of having just finished the race. Partly because half the world was watching. But mostly because I had accomplished my dream. The thrill is something you just never forget."

"Have you ever thought of selling it?" Carlos asked.

Stan tossed him a crazed look. "Are you on drugs or something? You heard what she just said. She'd never do that. I'm so sure."

"Whatever. I was just wondering—you know, if the economy got bad or something," Carlos said.

"No, Carlos. It's really much too important to me to part with," Rosie said. "You know, you work for years to fine-tune your skill. Then, when you qualify to represent our country in the Olympics, you've accomplished something to which few ever aspire. On top of that, you're competing against the best of the best in the world. And then to win is, well, like I said, it takes your breath away."

"I can't believe you brought it on the boat," Bruce said. He started to hand it to her, then pretended to drop it. "Oops!"

"Bruce . . . you klutz!" Vanessa said, placing her hands on her chest to catch her breath.

Bruce placed it with reverence into Rosie's hands.

"Thanks, Bruce. The truth is, you guys have been bugging me all semester long and I figured this would be the best way to get you off my case," Rosie said with a smile. "There. Are we happy campers now?"

She tucked the medal back into her purse.

Jodi made her way toward the front of the boat. She chose a spot away from the others, sat on the deck, removed her socks and shoes, then dangled her feet over the bow. She spent several quiet moments mesmerized by the water, which rolled out before her like a navy blue carpet. As far as she could see, nothing but gentle waves awaited their turn to splash against the ship's hull. The fresh spring air was intoxicating.

In the stillness of the moment, she leaned back on her left arm and began a silent prayer.

Lord, you brought me to this place for a reason. Sometimes it's hard for me to understand your ways. I can see that you put me in Kat's life as some kind of divine appointment. But we're so different. I hardly know what to say most of the time. And it's really easy for me to be judgmental. Please give me a love for her and the right words to share with her about you.

Jodi paused, her eyes following a pair of sea gulls flying inches above the water.

I could really use wisdom as I listen to Mrs. Meyer. She's far from you. But you love her just as you love me. Help me to have a heart of understanding. Speak to me now through your Word, I pray. In Jesus' name, amen.

She sat upright, reached into her rear pant pocket, and carefully retrieved the pocket Bible her dad had bought her last year. She turned to the fourth chapter of 1 John and placed her right forefinger to keep the pages from turning in the breeze as the boat sailed east in the middle of the bay.

When she came to verse five, it was as if the Lord was speaking directly to her about Mrs. Meyer: "They are of the world. Therefore they speak as of the world, and the world hears them. We are of God. He who knows God hears us; he who is not of God does not hear us." She sat back to consider the implication.

No wonder everyone else in the group, besides Heather and me, accepts Mrs. Meyer's ideas about tolerance, she thought. Even that little bit about "your God—whoever *she* may be" was a subtle twist of the truth.

Jodi continued her reading. When she got to verse eleven, the words virtually jumped off the page: "Beloved, if God so loved us, we also ought to love one another."

Ouch! Guess that includes Kat, she thought. *But how? I know I should love her, but it's another thing to know what that love looks like. And, if I'm totally honest, the whole thing scares me. I'm afraid of making a mistake—or maybe it's the fear of rejection.*

She read on. Her eyes widened as she read verse eighteen to the end of the chapter: "There is no fear in love; but perfect love casts out fear . . . We love Him because He first loved us. If someone says, 'I love God,' and hates his brother, he is a liar; for he who does not love his brother whom he has seen, how can he love God whom he has not seen? And this commandment we have from Him: that he who loves God must love his brother also."

Jodi was reading with such intense focus she didn't hear the footsteps that approached from behind.

"Jodi . . ."

Startled, she almost fell forward off the deck. She turned and saw Rosie standing over her.

"Hi, Mrs. Meyer." Jodi shielded her eyes as she looked up.

"What are you doing?"

"Like you said, I'm spending some time in reflection. Am I late for lunch?"

"No. Nothing like that. Would you mind telling me what you are reading?" Rosie put one hand on her hip.

"Oh, this? It's just my pocket New Testament."

Rosie took it from her, glanced at the well-worn pages, then handed it back. "I can appreciate your sincerity, Jodi. But let's put that away, dear."

"I don't understand . . ."

"In case you forgot—this *is* an official public-school trip. I don't think you're being considerate waving it around in plain view of the other students. Your thoughtless action may be offensive to others."

Jodi was at a loss of what to say, especially given Rosie's exaggeration. *I wasn't waving it at all*, she thought. "With all due respect, how is sitting here reading this little book . . ."

"All I'm asking you to be is considerate of other students, Jodi. Now I don't want to see that book again during the trip. If I do, you'll leave me no choice but to confiscate it until the end of the week. Am I understood?"

Jodi bit her lip, nodded, then tucked her Bible back into her pocket. This was a dark side of Rosie she hadn't seen before.

1:30 P.M.

During lunch, Jodi described to Heather her unexpected encounter with Mrs. Meyer over the Bible. Like Jodi, Heather thought Mrs. Meyer had acted unreasonably, but agreed it was better not to cause a scene. At the moment, the two friends sat beside each other for the afternoon session on tolerance. Rosie opened the discussion by inviting questions from Saturday's class.

"Yesterday, you said you no longer believe in a morality rooted in absolute truth. So what do you believe in now?" Heather asked, taking out her pen and notepad.

"I would say 'whatever works for you' is your 'truth.'"

"Come again?" Stan asked as he massaged his temples and then the back of his neck.

"We can plainly see throughout history that there have been different truths for different times. What worked two hundred years ago might not work today. So when it comes to truth, we each must find what works for us—and permit each other, out of fairness, to discover what works for them. That, in my book, is the heart of tolerance," Rosie said.

Stan's face betrayed the fact that he still didn't grasp her point. "So how do you handle right and wrong?" he asked.

"Good question. I've come to look at things in terms of choice," she said. "There are many choices in life, and I must decide what works best for me at this time."

Jodi thought, *Yeah, but not all consequences are equal. Some could kill us—like premarital sex and the risk of AIDS. Or is that moralizing?* This wasn't, after all, a debate situation. She kept her thoughts to herself, for now.

"It's just like in social studies," Carlos said, turning to Stan. "You know, as a society changes, 'truth' must flex with the times."

"Sounds like someone was actually paying attention in class." Rosie smiled.

"Yeah, live and let live, and all that," Kat said, playing with an earring.

"Speaking of living . . . how about we take a spin on one of those WaveRunners?" Bruce asked. He nodded toward the two dual-seat Yamaha crafts strapped along the side of the boat.

Rosie looked at her watch then held up a finger as if to say they'd take a break in a minute.

She continued. "Of course, there *may* be truth out there," Rosie pointed toward the sky. "But what that truth is we can't really know for sure."

"Sort of like the *X-Files*, huh?" Bruce pointed out. "'The truth is out there . . .'"

That's it, Jodi thought. Although she couldn't quite place the exact verse, the words that came to mind were unmistakable: "I am the way, the truth, and the life. No one comes to the Father except through Me." Truth. Plain as day. Spoken by Jesus, God's own Son.

All of her life Jodi believed that God was, first and foremost, a loving God. He didn't create mankind only to leave them guessing about truth and life-after-death questions.

What's more, Jodi guessed, deep down Mrs. Meyer knew what the truth was. Certainly somewhere in her Catholic upbringing she heard those words of Jesus—but Mrs. Meyer must not have liked the *claim* it made on her life. Was that why she had to dismiss, even discredit, Christianity? Perhaps that explained why Mrs. Meyer was so offended by her reading the Bible.

Jodi started to speak, slowly at first, like a turtle sticking its neck out of the safety of its shell. Especially with the memory of this morning's encounter still fresh in her mind.

"Mrs. Meyer?"

"Yes, Jodi?" Rosie raised an eyebrow.

"I don't mean to be disrespectful, but as I've been listening both yesterday and today, I think you've misrepresented people of faith." Her voice was clear and steady. Inside, her heart raced, much like it would during a tough debate—only this time, it pounded more than anything from her fear of being outspoken about her Christianity.

"Really? How so?" Rosie asked, her hands opened as if ready to receive a gift of insight, although her tone possessed a hint of sarcasm.

"Well, this might come as a surprise, but I don't stay up late at night thinking of ways to bash people of other faiths. In fact, I don't believe all other religions are wrong *all* of the time."

Rosie said, "Care to explain how that's possible?"

"Sure. For example, Jews, Muslims, and we Christians all believe there is just one God. We share a monotheistic view of God. But," Jodi inched farther out on the limb, "precisely *who* God is— now that's where we have a major disagreement."

Rosie managed a polite smile.

Jodi continued, her voice crisp. "See, Muslims believe Jesus was a prophet and a teacher. So do most Jews. But neither group believes Jesus was *also* God, and that he died for the sins of the world—and they'd *never* agree that he rose again from the dead. That's where a Christian parts company."

Rosie began to shuffle some papers on her lap.

Jodi sensed Mrs. Meyer's impatience, but as she studied the faces, Jodi was surprised to notice that Kat, who sat directly across from her, was actually listening. Heather was a different story. Jodi couldn't tell whether her friend was embarrassed—or praying. She pressed on.

"And, unlike the other world religions, which you lumped into a single box, Christianity is the only faith which views salvation as a free, undeserved gift. That's what God's grace is all about. We gain God's riches at Christ's expense. He was sacrificed in my place and paid the price for my sin—"

At that, Rosie cleared her throat and cut her off midsentence with a wave of her hand.

"I hate to interrupt you, Jodi. But we really do need to take a break," Rosie said with a glance at her watch.

"But I wasn't finished—"

"We've already spent more time on this subject than I had planned. And while you're entitled to your *opinion*," Rosie said, "we're all fellow travelers trying to discover our own way. What's most important is to 'live and let live.' I believe Kat made that observation."

Kat nodded.

"In the days ahead, let's make sure we respectfully accept all points of view rather than claim that a particular view is the correct one, which, in my experience, polarizes people," Rosie said speaking to the group, but clearly directing her comment toward Jodi.

Jodi felt a cloud of frustration cast a shadow on her spirit. *Why did the others get to express whatever they wanted? Why am I being singled out? Didn't Mrs. Meyer spend several minutes yesterday talking about her disappointment with her Catholic childhood? So why can't I express my view of faith in God?* Jodi wondered.

Jodi studied Rosie's face for a long, hard moment, trying to read her teacher's mind. Mrs. Meyer's face seemed tight, like the skin of a snare drum.

Rosie glanced down at her notes, avoiding Jodi's gaze.

"Okay, everyone. It's time for a break. You've got free time until dinner. Feel free to use the WaveRunners, and I believe the sliding board is an option too. Ask Phil to be sure."

9:37 P.M.

Jodi stepped into the cramped bathroom, placed her shampoo, conditioner, and soap into the narrow shower stall, turned back around, and closed the bathroom door. The lock was a primitive device, nothing more than an eyehook, which she raised and placed into the eyelet on the doorframe. *Might stop a gnat from entering,* she thought.

Phil had emphasized that showers were limited to four min-utes—every other day. The boat's fresh water supply was, unlike at home, considerably limited. Out of necessity they had to ration water for bathing if they were to make the week without stopping every day to replenish the supply.

She had no intention of exceeding the time limit—she couldn't endure any more scorn from the group. Her nerves were frazzled. She felt singled out by Rosie for her views, and she still was both-ered by that scene this morning on the deck. Why was reading a small Bible more offensive than Kat's reading about the Wicca reli-gion in her witchcraft book? Why didn't Rosie make Kat put her book away too?

Jodi stood before the tiny, scratched mirror and studied her face. Her thoughts drifted back to dinner.

Dinner—what a disaster zone.

Throughout the meal, several whispered and joked about her. Didn't they know she could hear every word? Or worse, maybe they didn't care that their verbal jabs hit below the belt. Their spiteful comments still echoed in her mind . . .

"Boy, has she got a Moses complex. She wants to lead us to the promised land—and there aren't any takers!"

"What a Jesus freak. Where does she get off?"

"Didn't she get the memo? This isn't church camp!"

"Yeah, for a minute I thought we were at a revival meeting."

"What was she thinking? Who can believe in a God that's so intolerant?"

"Too bad—she's cute—but she's whacked in the head."

Heather had made matters worse. *She even said I ought to back off. What's up with her?* Jodi wondered. *Why didn't she support me?*

Why didn't she counter their accusations? And this afternoon, she just sat in silence while Rosie slammed me—the people pleaser. No wonder she's on student council. Always knows when to speak and when to be politically correct. And she's supposed to be my best friend?

Jodi suppressed her tears. A moment alone. That's what she needed right now more than anything. She always enjoyed the soothing way a shower calmed her.

She pulled back the thin, tattered shower curtain, adjusted the temperature, and disrobed, placing her robe on a crooked nail on the wall, then stepped in. She'd indulge in a few minutes of peaceful escape from the meanspirited voices rattling around in her head.

The hot water felt good. She closed her eyes, took a deep breath, and let her facial pores drink up the moisture. She ran her fingers through her hair. Then, just as quickly as she began to relax, she stopped. Something about the water didn't feel quite right. It possessed a tacky quality as it touched her skin.

Puzzled, she opened her eyes.

Her mind tried to focus, to make sense out of what was happening. She was drenched by a blood red, sticky substance from the showerhead.

Her scream echoed across the bay.

Heather was the first to arrive.

"*Jodi!* Are you all right? What's the matter?" she called from the hallway.

When Jodi didn't answer, Heather rammed her shoulder against the door. The flimsy lock offered little resistance. She raced inside.

"Jodi? *Jodi!*"

Heather pulled back the shower curtain. Her face was hit with a blast of hot steam. Through the haze she managed to see Jodi slumped down in the corner, her body shrouded in a dark, red goo.

Heather gasped and quickly covered her mouth to contain a scream of her own.

With her free hand she grabbed the faucet and turned off the angry stream of water. She knelt beside Jodi, whose face was in her hands as she sobbed.

"What's going on? You hurt?" Heather demanded, almost hysterical. She lifted Jodi's chin to look her in the eyes.

Kat swooped into the bathroom and stood behind them.

"Is she okay?"

Heather pleaded, "Just hand me her robe—quickly!"

Kat grabbed Jodi's bathrobe off the hook on the wall and, along with a towel, handed them to Heather.

Aware that the others had crowded into the hallway outside of the door, Heather said, "Please, just give us some space—*and some privacy!*" She covered Jodi with the robe to escort her to her room.

After the girls left, Phil went into the bathroom, dismantled the showerhead, and discovered the remains of an opened, soggy packet of cherry Jell-O stuffed into the spout.

Heather walked Jodi through the main cabin in order to reach the spiral staircase up to their bunks. She saw Stan laughing by the kitchen sink. She guessed he was behind the practical joke.

Monday

8:17 A.M.

The smell of fresh-brewed coffee nudged Jodi awake. At home, that delicious aroma was part of her daily routine. Her dad, an early riser, started the day grinding his own beans—even steamed the milk into a frothy head that he'd add to the coffee once it finished percolating. But this wasn't home, and that wasn't her family clanking the dishes, chatting around the breakfast table.

The blend of sounds signaled she had overslept.

She lay motionless and remembered last night after the prank, after Phil assured her the shower was operating properly, how she returned to the bathroom, rinsed off the Jell-O, then crawled, humiliated by the whole ordeal, into her bunk. She had managed a feeble prayer then drifted into a restless sleep.

But the toughest part, by far, was yet to come—facing breakfast. Would they be watching her every move? Would they make fun of the way she reacted to last night's mischief? Or, worse, had someone planned another prank, like spiders in her drink? She covered her head with her pillow.

She considered skipping breakfast altogether. But if she did, whoever was responsible for the stunt would have won. They would have been successful in their attempt to rattle her self-confidence. The fighter in her didn't care to give them that satisfaction. No, she'd go to breakfast and put on a good face. She dressed in sweats, pulled her hair into a ponytail, tossed on a comfortable pair of sneakers, and made her way to the galley.

As she entered the front cabin, Phil was speaking.

"We're in for good weather today, even tomorrow. But according to what I've gathered from Coast Guard reports, chances are fairly strong for a midweek storm, maybe by Wednesday night, certainly no later than Thursday afternoon . . ."

He paused as Jodi made her way into the room, looking for an open seat.

Everyone looked in her direction but said nothing. An awkward moment passed before Bruce, who sat at one end of the table, asked Stan, positioned on the opposite end, "Could you please pass the Jell-O?"

Stan tried but failed to suppress a snicker.

Jodi's eyes darted between the two boys.

"Bruce, sometimes I just wanna bean you in the head," Heather said evenly. She pulled out the empty chair next to her and beckoned Jodi to join them.

"Good morning . . . how'd ya rest?"

"Just fine, thanks." She took a seat then poured herself some coffee. The atmosphere in the room remained tense. She ignored the sensation.

"You were saying there's a storm headed our way?" Jodi asked, her voice pleasant. She reached for the French toast.

Phil picked up where he left off. "It appears so. Storms this time of year are not unusual. But the Coast Guard indicated this one could get ugly before it's over."

"How bad could things be? It's not like we're on the ocean," Carlos said. His voice wavered, lacking conviction.

"Actually, the waves could reach as high as eight to ten feet even in the bay, and that, I'm afraid, is more than we should attempt to navigate," Phil said. "At that height, this boat would be tossed around like a yo-yo." He spoke the words without fear, just the cold facts.

Rosie shifted in her seat. "Do you think we should cut the trip short, hon?"

"We'll be all right. I've charted a course that will return us close to our departure point by Wednesday. If things turn nasty, barring any unforeseen complications, we can make shore, no problem." He gave her a wink.

Rosie didn't press Phil on his judgment.

"Now, if you'll excuse me. The anchor mechanism didn't retrieve fully this morning. I've got work to do down below," Phil said. He refilled his coffee mug and left.

"Nothing like a little excitement to keep us on our toes," Rosie said cheerfully. "We'll begin our morning session at nine, all right?" She rose to leave. A moment later Carlos, then Stan, excused themselves too.

It was Bruce and Justin's turn to clean up after the meal. They collected the used cups, plates, and silverware with unusual speed then washed and dried them in the galley area. Vanessa, Kat, and Heather lingered at the table in the gathering room as Jodi finished her breakfast.

"I couldn't help but notice the book you were reading yesterday," Vanessa said to Kat. "Looked fascinating. What's it about?"

"You mean my book on the Wiccan religion?"

Vanessa nodded.

"Oh, that. Well, it's kinda hard to summarize." Kat paused to steal a glance at Jodi and Heather. "I really don't want to offend anyone."

"Go on, girl. I'm sure we can all handle it."

Kat continued. "See, a friend who knows I've always had an interest in the spirit world thought I might want to look into Wicca."

Jodi had some idea of what might be coming. When she and Kat unpacked on Saturday, Jodi, who loved to read, couldn't help but notice that several of Kat's books were an introduction to witch-craft. Kat offered to let Jodi thumb through them. She declined, explaining what she knew of the Wicca faith represented the exact opposite of what she believed.

Kat continued. "As far as I can tell, the Wicca religion is a blend of feminism, environmentalism, and liberalism—three things I happen to be passionate about."

"So am I," Vanessa said with interest.

Kat cleared her throat. "Well, that's what first attracted me. The Wiccan also believes we should live in harmony with nature because we're really not some kind of special creation, you know, made in the image of God and all that debatable stuff."

She paused and looked at Jodi and Heather. When neither spoke, she said, "Instead, we're just part of the vast oneness of the universe. We were not created any different than the water, the fish, the trees . . ."

As Bruce cleared Jodi's plate, he said, "Sounds like these Wicca people believe we're nothing more than large road kill!"

"I don't think you're a part of this discussion," Vanessa said.

"Hey, lighten up. It was just a joke," Bruce said.

Jodi couldn't resist. She asked, "So if we're just blobs of human-ity made from the same particle matter as Pluto, what do they say about sin and good and evil?"

"From what I've read so far, Wiccans don't believe in the con-cept of sin because, for there to be sin, you'd have to believe in a God who created humans above the rest of nature."

"I'm not sure I'm following," Vanessa said.

"Here's the example the book used," Kat said. "It asks, Can a dog sin? No. How about a bird—can it sin? No. Since we humans are just part of the general creation—we're made from the same stuff as the dog and the bird—we don't sin, either."

"Give me a break," Jodi said under her breath.

"Come on, Jodi, just let her talk," Heather said firmly.

Jodi rolled her eyes.

"Hey, like I said, I'm still just exploring what it's all about."

Although Bruce and Justin were drying the glasses in the galley, they followed the discussion. "What about those apes who killed Justin's mom and dad?" Bruce asked.

Kat turned around to face him. "What about them?"

"Well, would the Wiccans say that was wrong, or evil?"

"That depends."

"You're kidding, right?" Bruce said. "You can't be serious."

"No offense, Justin," Kat said, "but if his parents violated the laws established by that society for their country, then it would have been his parents' own fault. His parents decided to go there. They knew the risks—"

Bruce was indignant. "You're one cold fish, Kat."

"I didn't say I agree with the Wiccan viewpoint. I'm just giving you what I think they'd argue," Kat said defensively.

Jodi cut in. "So you haven't learned how to cast any spells yet, I suppose?"

Kat missed the sarcasm. "No. But I did learn Wicca teaches its magic exists for positive purposes, you know, like to promote stuff like healing and guidance and, ya know, positive energy. It's way different than Satanism 'cause a Wiccan witch practices white magic."

"Well, looks like I'm in the wrong pew," Jodi said wryly.

Heather shot her a nasty look. "She just said their spells are for the *benefit* of mankind. What's wrong with that? And why are you so down on her?"

Jodi bristled. She could understand how Vanessa, an unbeliever, might be tempted to explore Kat's ideas. But what possessed Heather to do the same? Was she that blind to what Kat was saying? How could she reconcile such ridiculous talk with her Christianity? Or was this just another occasion when Heather didn't want to rock the boat?

Without thinking, Jodi fired back. "Well fine, Kat—if you want to believe that nonsense and spend eternity apart from God, it's your choice. Who am I to stop you? Go right ahead." The instant she spoke, she knew her words were reckless, devoid of love. Her face flushed.

A stiff moment passed between them.

"I . . . wow . . . listen to me . . ." Jodi fumbled for the right words to apologize. "Where did that come from?"

The others, stunned by her outburst, didn't move.

Jodi's right hand reached out toward Kat in what was intended to be a loving gesture. "Kat, I'm so *very* sorry. That was really, really wrong of me."

"I'll say it was," Rosie said, angered.

Jodi guessed Mrs. Meyer must have caught the tail end of the exchange when she entered the room for the nine o'clock session.

Rosie put her right hand on her hip. "Jodi, your behavior and attitude are way out of line. It runs contrary to the spirit of what we're attempting to accomplish this week. Hasn't anything we've discussed registered?"

If there had been a way for the earth to open up and swallow her, Jodi would have gladly welcomed the option.

10:47 A.M.
Huntingdon Valley, Pennsylvania

Amy Schultz maneuvered her white 1997 Ford Escort into the rear parking lot of Huntingdon Valley High School. No matter how slowly she negotiated the speed bumps, each painted school-bus yellow, they managed to reach up and scrape the bottom of her muffler. She winced as the last of three bumps made its mark on the belly of her car.

The lot was empty, except for a few utility pickup trucks used by the janitorial service. She parked with the precision of a driver ed instructor, engaged the emergency brake, then checked her watch. She was pleased that she still had just over ten minutes to locate the principal's office. He had told her to use the staff entrance adjacent to the cafeteria loading dock. She could see it clearly from where she sat.

She gathered her purse and a photo that was placed inside a white envelope. With her hand on the door handle, she stopped for just an instant. Was she overreacting? She had called her husband, Michael, to share her misgivings. He, as usual, said to do what she thought best. He wasn't unsympathetic, but this, as he reminded her, wasn't the first time their son was missing, and it probably wouldn't be the last.

Her woman's intuition wouldn't let it go. She stepped out of the car, locked the door with a beep, then headed inside the school.

"John Crans." The principal of Huntingdon Valley High extended his hand and drew Amy into his office in one smooth, welcoming motion. "You must be Amy Schultz. Pleased to meet you."

"Thanks for seeing me on such short notice."

"Here, have a seat." John pointed to a chair facing his large, wood desk. He slid several stacks of file folders to the side then leaned against the front edge of the desk.

"Pardon the mess. The school board meets in a few days, and I'm swimming in paperwork," he said. "We're all racing to hit the deadline."

His secretary tapped lightly on the door. "Excuse me, Mr. Crans," she said then continued without waiting for a reply, "I need your signature on this purchase order."

He rose, signed the document, then circled behind his desk and sat in his brown, padded chair. "It may be spring break, but the staff keeps me hopping." He smiled then rolled up his sleeves and leaned forward.

"I know you're very busy. This will only take a minute."

"Glad to be of whatever help I can," John said.

"Well, to make a long story short, my husband, Michael, and I have a student enrolled here. He's our son. Actually, he's not officially our son . . . What I mean to say is we treat him as if he were our son and we hope to adopt him someday."

"So you're his foster parents, correct?"

"Yes. We've only had him for a few months, but already we feel like he's our own."

"What's his name?"

"Justin."

John slid back, picked a pen out of the center drawer of his desk, and scribbled a few notes on a yellow legal pad.

"Justin Schultz . . . which grade is he in?"

"Actually, it would be Justin Moore since we haven't finalized the adoption. Eleventh grade. He's sixteen."

"Do you know the name of his homeroom teacher?"

"Yes, I seem to recall it's Mr. Burdick."

"I believe you mean Bornick," John said.

"*Bornick*. I see. Justin doesn't really communicate much about such things. He's a quiet kid. Keeps to himself most of the time. Don't get me wrong—as a family, we really do get along just fine. I've got a picture here if that helps." Amy offered to hand it to him.

He glanced at the photo, then set it aside. "First things first. What exactly is the nature of your concern? Are his grades slipping? Is he having problems with another student?"

"No. He does fine academically. Like I said, he keeps his own company. He has one best friend, Ron Davis. Oh . . . and there are a few guys he practices martial arts with in the gym. That's the problem."

"Martial arts?"

"No, Ron Davis. Ron does just about everything with Justin. In fact, it's not unusual for Justin to spend a couple nights in a row at Ron's house—sometimes without telling us."

John listened patiently.

"When Justin didn't come home the last few nights, we assumed he was with Ron. But when Ron called wondering where Justin has been the last couple of days, we were alarmed."

John ran his left hand through his hair. "When did you get that call?"

"Last night," Amy said, her face flushed with worry.

He consulted his tablet. "Let me see if I've got this straight. Justin's best friend, Ron, called last evening—"

"That's right, Sunday night."

"And Ron said it had been several days since he had seen Justin. That takes us back to Friday, or maybe Thursday, right?"

"Correct."

"When was the last time you saw Justin?"

"I think Friday morning, breakfast, that was the last time."

"Forgive me for being blunt, Mrs. Schultz, but why don't you go to the police? I believe they handle missing persons a whole lot more efficiently than the school system."

Amy fidgeted with her hands. "We don't want there to be any marks against our parenting record."

John gave her a puzzled look. "How's that?"

Amy folded her hands. "When you want to adopt a foster child, the state weighs many factors, such as 'Do you have the resources to provide the proper care?' 'Do you have adequate living space?' For obvious reasons, if the child in your care ends up missing—well, you get the picture. We care deeply for him and want to provide him with a good home environment. He's been through a lot of pain in his life—"

"So what specifically can I do for you at this juncture?"

"I'm wondering if we might take a peek inside his locker to see if there's anything that might explain his absence."

John rubbed his chin. Running a school of 2,209 students already taxed all of his energies. He didn't get paid enough to play private detective on the side just because some worrywart couldn't keep track of her own kid. Besides, he really needed to complete the report for the board.

He looked at Amy Schultz. Just another parent trying to do her best raising a kid in this crazy world. Why not take a few minutes to help? Of course, if the American Civil Liberties Union got wind of it, they'd blast both him and the school with a wrongful search and invasion of privacy lawsuit in a heartbeat.

"Mrs. Schultz, I can see you're very concerned about Justin's welfare. But I'm sure you can appreciate that there are certain hoops the school must jump through before searching a student's locker, especially where there is no prior notice given to the student and no indication he or she would be a threat to the safety of the other students."

She swallowed hard and nodded.

"Here's the best I can do. I'll consult with our legal expert this afternoon—he's probably gone to lunch already—and make sure we're not inviting a lawsuit. If you'll give me your number, I'll call you once I have that opinion. If he says it's a go, fine. I'll arrange a time with you, maybe as early as this afternoon around five, and we'll take a look. How's that?"

Amy smiled and nodded.

"I really appreciate anything you can do for us. Thank you for your time, Mr. Crans." She jotted down her name and home number then rose to leave.

1:36 P.M.
Chesapeake Bay, Maryland

The students gathered for their afternoon session. Rosie, who was the last to arrive, took her seat.

"Sorry I'm late," Rosie said. "I was checking with Phil about the anchor situation. You've probably noticed he's been working in the hull most of the day trying to correct the problem he described this morning. He asked if two of the guys would give him a hand after this session. Justin and Stan, would you help?"

They nodded. "If you need muscles, you came to the right place," Stan said. He flexed his biceps.

"Thank you. Before we begin, how's everybody doing?"

"Mrs. Meyer?"

"Yes, Bruce."

"Is there any chance Phil can swing us by a harbor somewhere for just a few minutes—I've got to check how the Flyers are doing. They may have skated into the finals."

"I second the idea," Stan said. "And I'd like to see if the Sixers are still ahead in their division. Besides, I think I'm starting to get the shakes from TV withdrawal." He pretended to experience a muscle spasm.

They laughed.

Rosie smiled. "That's not an option, guys. I'm confident you'll be just fine. Any other comments?" She waited a moment. "Okay, let's get started. This afternoon, I'm going to present a real-life situa-tion you may have heard about in the news. Then, I'd like for you to dis-cuss the various issues it raises in light of our emphasis on tolerance."

She consulted her notes. "Here are the facts. A seventeen-year-old girl who attended a school in Philadelphia learned she was pregnant. She wasn't married, she didn't intend to marry the boy with whom she had had sex, and she didn't want to have the baby."

Rosie glanced around. Everyone was focused, except Justin. Why was he so distracted? So distant most of the time? Sure, he had shared about his parents' murder the first night; then again, maybe he had opened up more than he wanted. Rosie couldn't shake her misgivings about him. She had the odd sensation he was hiding something, some secret from the group. But what?

She looked at her notes. "As she struggled with her options, she approached her school guidance counselor for advice. He, in turn, strongly advised that she have an abortion. But there was one problem. In Pennsylvania, a minor must notify her parents before undergoing that procedure."

"I remember hearing about this," Carlos said.

"I'm not surprised," Rosie said. "It was blown into a big case because the counselor made arrangements for her to be transported out of state, to New Jersey—during school hours—where she could get an abortion without notifying her parents."

"Yeah, and didn't he help pay for it too?" Vanessa asked.

"Not exactly. He helped her arrange for the necessary money. Here's the twist. Afterward, both her boyfriend and her parents discovered what happened and planned to sue the school for undermining their rights," Rosie said.

"What rights did the boyfriend have?" Bruce asked.

"Yo, space case," Stan said. "It takes two to tango, right?" He winked. "The baby—"

"Fetus," Rosie interjected.

"—whatever, was half his," Stan said.

"Got it," said Bruce.

"Those are the facts. Now, let's dissect the issues from several angles: the parents, the counselor, the boy and girl involved, the law, freedom of choice, or the larger matter of abortion rights in general. As you weigh in your opinion," she said as she ventured a look at Jodi, "let's remember the basic principle of tolerance: mutual respect of all points of view. Who wants to start?"

Vanessa raised her hand then said, "I'd take exception to Stan's comment, you know, when he said it was like, 50 percent the guy's baby. Come on, it was 100 percent her *body*. Her body, her choice. She should have the last say over what happens to her body." She looked around for support among the other girls. Kat was nodding. Heather appeared open but noncommittal.

"But wasn't she wrong to try and do an end run around the parental notification thing?" Stan asked.

Kat said, "Depends. If the law is unjust—"

"Who's to say what's unjust?" Stan asked, his voice taking on a more serious tone.

"Well, if in her view the law wasn't fair, then it was unjust—that's her truth," Kat said.

Jodi jumped in. "Wait a minute. Are you saying any time we don't like a law, we should just find a way around it? We can simply ignore the established authority?"

Heather, sitting to the left of Jodi, turned and said, "It sounds like she's saying in this situation this girl was penalized because of where she lived. If she lived in New Jersey, she could have chosen to have an abortion without her parents' permission and that would have been perfectly legal. So the truth, in her eyes, was that Pennsylvania's law was intolerant of her rights."

Once again, Jodi found herself puzzled by Heather's wishy-washy logic but decided against going head-to-head with her in public.

"How about the counselor? Should he be fined or, worse, fired for his role?" Rosie asked.

Carlos said, "No. He was just following his convictions. Why should he be punished for that? In his mind he was battling against—"

"The law of the land," Jodi interjected.

"Maybe, but it was a bad law, an unjust law at best," Carlos said. "He did the compassionate thing by helping her."

"So who decides what justice is?" Rosie asked.

"Society—whatever they think is just, that's justice. Which, as we know, can change over time," Vanessa said.

Jodi pressed her. "But isn't that exactly what the law represents? The elected officials passing laws based on the will of the people?"

Vanessa shook her head in disagreement. "They pass laws based on some biased preconceived notion—worse, they pass laws for what their rich lobbyist buddies want."

Rosie intervened. "Does it seem to anyone besides me that the law was intolerant of her right to choose? That is, after all, a fundamental right for women."

Jodi felt caught in the cross fire. She shot back. "Wait a minute. Our Founding Fathers *never* said anything in the Constitution about a right to choose. They mention specifically a right to bear arms, to vote, to own property, to enjoy religious freedom—"

Vanessa cut her off. "Yeah. They wrote the Constitution to preserve those freedoms—*if* you had the right skin color. Face it, girl, most of the Founding Fathers were hypocritical slave owners."

Rosie didn't give Jodi a chance to respond. "As you well know, Jodi, that was two hundred years ago. Humanity has come of age. The times have changed, and so must our social conventions. That's why the U.S. Supreme Court expanded upon the narrowness of the Constitution in their 1973 *Roe v. Wade* decision, which established the right to privacy. That includes the right of a woman to privately choose what she does with her body."

"So you believe *all* women have this right to choose?" Jodi asked, setting her up with a debate tactic.

"Absolutely. Without question," Rosie said. She folded her arms.

"Don't you mean 50 percent of all women have this right?"

"What are you driving at?" Rosie said cautiously.

"Well, in fact, roughly 50 percent of babies who are aborted are girls. Using your logic, shouldn't those girls have a right to choose what happens to *their* bodies? Doesn't an abortion rob them of that cherished right?"

The eyes of everyone were instantly glued on Rosie.

Rosie began to say something then stopped.

Stan said, "I feel like I'm sitting at a tennis match, watching the pros battle the ball back and forth, you know? And Jodi, you got brains and looks, what a combo pack."

Jodi was unsure how to receive the compliment.

After an awkward moment, Stan said, "I think I understand what Jodi's driving at."

Rosie gestured for him to continue. Jodi looked at Stan, surprised.

"Take our football team. Say one player chose to wander off the field and help an old lady cross the street, okay? And let's say he chose to do that in the middle of a game—duh! As noble as his desire to help the old lady might be, his choice still affects other people . . . Besides, Coach Thomas would kick his sorry butt off the team for leaving the field!"

They all laughed.

Jodi was pleasantly impressed by Stan's example. *Maybe he's not a dumb jock after all*, she thought.

"Exactly," Jodi said. "Your teammate isn't choosing to act in a vacuum. Society is just like that. My choice can affect people besides myself, so I have a moral obligation to do the right thing." Jodi fidgeted with her hair as she thought about a way to illustrate her point. "Okay, for example, the choice to drink alcohol—and get drunk—in the privacy of my own home affects those in my house. That choice affects others. See what I mean?" She looked at Mrs. Meyer with a kind smile. Surely Mrs. Meyer would have to agree, since her dad was an alcoholic.

Rosie put down the pen she was twirling in her hand. "I can see why you won first place on our debate team, Jodi. You make your point very well."

For the first time all week, Jodi felt some small measure of affirmation from her teacher.

"And yet," Rosie was quick to add, "you keep introducing morality into the equation. We've already discussed the fact that matters of morality, unfortunately, are rooted in religion. And religion, in turn, divides people."

Jodi said, "But, Mrs. Meyer—"

"If I may finish?" Rosie said firmly. "Unlike the narrowness of religion, tolerance is compassionate because it encourages the celebration of our diversity. It allows the individual to be free to embrace what works best for him or her—as long as it does no harm to the environment or the common good of society."

"Mrs. Meyer," Jodi said evenly, "what you've just described has a name."

"I'm sorry, I'm not sure what you're referring to," Rosie said, her brow furrowed into an intense knot.

"When a society removes God from the picture and, instead, elevates man as the measure of all things, it's called secular humanism. And that's a religious view."

Carlos turned to Jodi. "Call it what you want. But it seems to me that tolerance is about accepting *all* points of view, in art, science, sexual orientation . . ."

"Don't forget political ideology and multiculturalism," Vanessa added.

Jodi was itching to debate the point further. Why do some schools celebrate lesbian motherhood with textbooks like *Heather Has Two Mommies* but deny curriculum that celebrates abstinence and monogamy? What about evolution? Why did their school teach the theory of evolution as *fact*, but exclude the Creation story?

What happened to accepting all points of view? she wondered.

4:44 P.M.
Huntingdon Valley, Pennsylvania

"Mrs. Schultz? John Crans over at the high school."

"Thank you for calling, Mr. Crans." Amy had snatched the phone on the first ring. She tried not to sound too anxious. "What did you find out?"

"I spoke with legal about your request. I'm told this is one of those gray areas . . . you know, student rights versus school property issues. It's kind of a sticky situation," he paused.

"I see . . ."

"At the same time"—she heard him shuffle a few papers— "ah, here it is. He explains that—and I'm quoting from his note, 'Because the school district is the sole owner of the locker, which we do not rent or sell; nor do we in any other way transfer ownership rights to the student beyond the convenience of use,' end quote, we *may* be on safe ground."

Amy gripped the phone tightly. "Does that mean we can take a look inside?"

"What it means is I'm still at risk should the ACLU get wind of the search and decide they've got nothing better to do than stick their collective noses into the matter."

Her heart sank. "I understand."

"You can always tell when it's Christmas or Easter in the school district. You'll see a flock of the ACLU boys hovering like vultures over the building ready to pounce on some scrap of injudiciousness."

"I certainly don't want to get the school into hot water. It's just difficult for me to think there might be some clue . . . a note, or maybe, I don't know, some indication as to where my Justin might be sitting there inside of his locker." Amy switched the phone to her right shoulder, swallowed hard, then sighed into the phone.

"Ah, forget about 'em. I've been in education for twenty-seven years and I've had my fill of looking over my shoulder. Tell you what I'm prepared to do," John said.

"Yes?" she said, expectant.

"It's almost five o'clock already, and I was just handed a stack of papers that need my review and signature. Why don't you wait and see if Justin comes home tonight. Maybe he just went camping over the weekend. If he's still not home by the morning, give me a call and we'll go take a look. How does that sound?"

In truth she wanted to demand that he open the locker that evening. Justin was missing, and that's all that mattered. But figuring Mr. Crans's offer was not negotiable, she decided not to press the matter.

"Mr. Crans, you have no idea how much I appreciate this," Amy said.

11:53 P.M.

The moonlight's reflection danced softly across the bay. The occupants of the houseboat were lost deep in the first waves of sleep, having retired an hour ago—everyone, that is, but one.

With care, he peeled back his covers, sat up in his bunk, and listened. Besides the snoring from his roommate, the only other sound came from the boat itself. A ripple of creaks and groans echoed as its aging body remained suspended in place against the unseen pull of the tide.

A thread of light from the crescent moon did little to illuminate the dark shadows in his room. He remained motionless yet expectant, long enough for his eyes to adjust to the darkness. The time to act had come. He was convinced the heavy burden he had carried for so many years, yes, the pain he worked to conceal, would at long last be lifted through this final, desperate act.

It struck him how life and death were such a mystery. Now that he stood on the threshold of death's door, he felt oddly alive. Maybe it was the fact that there was no reversing what he was about to do . . . no rewind button to push . . . no reset button to restore reality after the fact.

For an instant, he hesitated. A face came to his mind.

Jodi. She was different than the others. What was that brightness in her eyes? Why was she so self-assured? What was the source of her inner strength? Surely she's experienced pain, disappointment, and despair. Anyone could see how Mrs. Meyer bore down on her—yet Jodi always bounced back.

Jodi.

Would she scream or call out to God? Probably both, he decided.

The others would scream too—of that he was sure. But he doubted they would call on a God they didn't believe existed. Would God listen if they did?

He shook his head as if somehow the motion would stop the steady flood of thought. Just a waste of time.

He lifted his legs over the edge of the bunk and placed his feet silently onto the floor. With a slow, smooth motion, he lifted his frame from the bunk, stood, and waited to see if his roommate had somehow awakened.

Confident his movements remained unnoticed, he noiselessly moved across the room, stooped down into the recesses of the corner, and slipped his hand into the denim backpack. A bead of perspiration began to form along his forehead. With the back of his left hand, he wiped away the sweat.

There wasn't anything he could do to throttle the racing of his heartbeat.

Behind him, the snoring stopped.

He froze, still hunched over the bag, his right hand gripping the knife. If discovered, he'd have to halt his plan. The element of surprise was absolutely essential. Any unusual sound—even a bit of conversation with his roommate at this hour—brought with it the possibility Phil would be roused from his sleep down the hall.

With Phil in the picture, everything changed.

He couldn't take that risk.

He waited.

In the top bunk, his roommate rolled over. But in the absence of light, he couldn't tell whether this new sleeping position was facing away from or toward him.

The sweat reappeared on his brow.

Did his roommate hear the pounding within his chest? Was he awake? Even if he was, could he have seen the knife? Unlikely. Not from that position. Maybe his eyes were adjusting to the murkiness too. *Can he see the outline of my body?* he wondered.

Just in case, he began to ease his grip on the knife.

The past two nights, the endless snoring from his roommate had filled the room. What caused the drone to stop tonight? He couldn't remain in this awkward position for much longer.

Frustrated by this development yet unwilling to jeopardize his plan, he tucked the blade under several garments in his bag, retraced his steps, and climbed back into bed.

For now.

Tuesday
Huntingdon Valley, Pennsylvania

9:17 A.M.

"Good morning, Mr. Crans. I hope you're not on a diet," Amy Schultz said as she presented a fresh box of Cinnabon's cinnamon rolls. "Here, these are for you."

He lifted the lid and took a whiff. "Mrs. Schultz, you really didn't have to go to this trouble," John Crans said, lingering over the heavenly aroma. "At the same time, I fully intend to enjoy one with coffee after we finish. Thank you."

She returned his smile.

They were standing outside of Mr. Crans's office, waiting on the janitor. "If you don't mind, I'll just set this out of harm's way in my office," Mr. Crans said, then quickly ducked inside.

A moment later, he stepped out empty-handed and pulled the door closed behind him. As he did, he saw the school janitor approaching.

"Mrs. Schultz, I'd like for you to meet Frank Reed. He's our head janitor, which really means he has more access around this school than I," John Crans said with a good-natured laugh.

"Pleased to meet you," she said, shaking Frank's hand.

"Frank, I need you to open locker 117B in the west wing."

"No problem."

They walked in silence across the freshly waxed, white-tiled floor, turned down the first hall, then slowed their pace to study the numbers riveted to the surface of the lockers. Frank's oversized key ring rattled at his side as he shuffled behind the others, his body leaning slightly to one side as if bearing the weight of an unseen heavy object.

The lockers, narrow metal compartments stacked two high, lined the walls on both sides of the hallway. Each was outfitted with a combination lock the student could set. Just below the black dial with white lettering was a small keyhole that permitted the master key to bypass the combination. This design was both a security precaution and a means for the school to open a locker in the event a student forgot his or her sequence of numbers.

"Here we go," Frank said. He sorted through his keys, found the appropriate one, bent over, and unlocked the door on the lower locker. He swung it open.

"Need anything else, Mr. Crans?"

"That should do it," John said. "Stop by my office in about fifteen minutes—I'll share a treat with you, compliments of Mrs. Schultz."

Frank smiled with appreciation, turned, and left, whistling as he walked away.

"I'll let you do the honors, Mrs. Schultz."

Amy wasn't sure what to look for as she lowered herself in front of her son's locker. She began to reach forward then hesitated as an uncomfortable feeling gnawed away at her conscience.

Would Justin resent her for violating his space? After all, she'd only been his foster mother for a few months. And, as if that weren't enough, teens were always so indignant about their privacy. She couldn't blame him. To be a teenager was to exist in the no man's land somewhere between childhood and adulthood. He was still dependent on her for most everything—food, clothing, car and health insurance—and, in that regard, she had a right and a responsibility to care for his welfare. Even if it meant snooping around?

"I think Justin will understand, don't you?" she asked, as if the principal was privy to her internal debate.

Mr. Crans leaned against the adjacent locker. "Hey, I'd probably do the same thing if I were in your position."

She removed his notebook and assortment of textbooks one at a time, examining each one slowly, with great care as if its pages might contain a priceless treasure. When nothing worthwhile was evident, she added it to the stack on the floor.

"There's nothing," she said, deflated as she stood to face him.

"I'm sorry, Mrs. Schultz. Can't say we didn't try." John was about to close the door but decided to glance in for himself. "Did you take a look at his gym bag?"

"Well, I . . . I didn't really notice it." She swung back down to see where he was pointing. She had been so focused on the books, she completely overlooked the bag as it hung from a hook in the back. She took it down, unzipped it, and began to scrutinize the contents.

A martial arts book . . . his Nikes . . . a dirty, gray hand towel . . . his school-issued gym shorts and T-shirt . . . two discarded candy wrappers . . . and a crumpled-up piece of scrap paper.

"What's this?" She stood to take advantage of the light then smoothed out the crinkled page in her hand. The note was as startling as it was cryptic. John leaned over her shoulder as she read it out loud: "*Someone is gonna die on that trip! Meet me behind the gym after school. Alone.*"

"It's not signed," John said.

"No date, either." She looked at him for a long moment. "What trip?"

1:18 P.M.
Chesapeake Bay, Maryland

"Jodi, sometimes I wonder why you're so, like . . . well, so militant," Heather said. Her face appeared strained. Lunch was over and they, as the last to finish, lingered at the table before taking their turn to clean up.

Jodi smirked. "Guess I was just made that way."

"I'm being serious, Jodi."

"So what are you saying, Heather? That I'm insensitive?"

Heather nodded. "You totally dogged Mrs. Meyer this morning."

Jodi thought back to the session. "Okay, I'll admit it. I had enough of her manipulation of the truth. I just spoke up for what I believe. I wasn't disrespectful or anything—"

Heather interrupted. "That's not how I heard it. Let me see, you said something like 'I'm sick of this propaganda. You don't want the truth to be told, do you, Mrs. Meyer? You can't handle the truth so you bury it underneath six feet of muddled thinking.' I'm not sure I'd call that respectful."

Jodi sipped a soda. "I thought tolerance was a two-way street. Every time I disagree with this live-and-let-live, every-man-picks-his-own-truth mantra, Mrs. Meyer shuts me down, ya know?"

"Maybe because your approach is not exactly the best way to win friends," Heather said after a moment. "Sometimes you just gotta let stuff ride. You know, be cool." Heather crossed her legs.

Jodi looked Heather in the eyes for a long moment. "We've been friends for how long? Three years, right?"

Heather nodded.

"So don't take this the wrong way, okay? This whole trip you seem to be a real people pleaser. I don't see you taking a stand for what you believe. You know, for the truth . . . for God," Jodi said. "Half the time I wonder why you don't speak up. And you know what I think?" She didn't wait for a response. "It all comes down to applause, Heather. You live for other people's applause."

"So what if I do?" Heather asked. She folded her arms.

"Put it this way. Ever watch those old rock stars on VH1, the ones who aren't popular anymore and how they talk about their career back in the eighties or whenever?"

"You mean the *Behind the Music* specials?"

"Yeah. It's like they all lived for the sex and backstage parties, right? That, plus the applause." Jodi tucked her hair behind her right ear then said, "One night the lead singer from some band—I don't remember which—confessed that without the screaming fans they felt lost. The crowds weren't snatching up their CDs. In fact, if you can even find their music, it's probably in the used CD section at MediaPlay."

"Um, you've lost me—"

"My point is that you and I are no different. All of us want to be accepted. We want to be liked—to fit in. When we don't have that admiration, we get depressed. Am I right?"

"Sure, but who doesn't?"

"Okay, what I'm trying to say is you're kinda like those rock stars, always living for the approval from people, see what I mean? And that's a dead end."

"So?"

"Aren't we supposed to be different, you know, as Christians? We can live for the praise from friends or from God. Remember when our pastor said that we should live our lives before an audience of One?"

Heather shook her head no. "I must have slept in that day."

"Well, his point was that God's approval is what we should care about most. And that got me thinking: Do I want God's applause more than anything?"

"Yeah, but what about getting along with others right here on good old earth?"

"Honestly?"

Heather nodded.

"Frankly, Heather, it's not that important to me. If other people like me, great. But most of the people you work so hard to impress, you'll never see again after we graduate next year. Poof!" She snapped her fingers. "In a flash they'll be gone. So will our opportunity to be Jesus to them. I'd rather have them think I was a dork or even get a low grade from Mrs. Meyer but please God by taking a stand for what I know is true."

Heather started to stack the dirty plates in front of her.

"Aren't you overreacting just a little? Don't you think being a Christian is a personal matter?" Heather asked. "You know, between you and God? Besides, maybe God didn't make me like you."

Jodi shook her head in disagreement. "My faith in God isn't some kind of spiritual fire insurance. I don't keep it locked away in a safe at home so when I die it'll keep me out of hell."

"So I'm supposed to be some kind of saint . . . like *you*?"

Jodi ran her hand through her hair. "Hey, I'm not picking on you, Heather. And I never said I was perfect. To me faith is a lifelong process of becoming more like Jesus . . . and I've got a long way to go. What I'm trying to say is my love for him affects everything, ya know? That includes my choices and my relationships in this life."

Heather started to look away.

"And yes, to me being a Christian is both a personal and a public matter," Jodi said, then placed a hand on Heather's arm and gave it a friendly squeeze. "Jesus took a stand for me on the cross—how could I do any less for him?"

"You just have more guts than I do, I guess," Heather said looking her in the eyes.

"Hey, this doesn't take guts. It's not like I'm being asked to give blood or anything like that—and you know how I hate hospitals and needles—so don't get me started!"

2:00 P.M.

"Okay, everybody, listen up." Rosie stood next to the twelve-foot fiberglass sliding board on the back deck of the ship as she spoke. Rosie had surprised the group thirty minutes prior by announcing she was suspending the afternoon class in favor of cliff diving, prompted in part by the news from Phil that the storm alert was now moved up to Wednesday.

Rosie sensed some of the students were getting cabin fever and felt this activity would do them some good. Besides, she figured this might be their last chance to take advantage of the beautiful weather. Those interested had changed into their swimsuits and stood awaiting further instructions.

"This morning Phil scoped out the safest place for us to dive—which is between that large pine tree"—she pointed to the left atop the bluff on the shoreline—"and that clump of scrub brush to the right of it. I'm going to ask you to stay within those boundaries, all right?"

Bruce, Carlos, Jodi, and Kat nodded.

"I believe Vanessa and Heather have decided to use the Wave-Runners, and Stan and Justin are staying on board with Phil to finish their work on the anchor," Rosie said. "They'll join us when they're finished. Questions?"

"How can you be so sure diving from those bluffs is safe?" Carlos asked.

"Phil was a Navy Seal, remember?" Rosie said with a supportive smile. "Earlier this morning he swam along the coast and confirmed the depth of the bay and the absence of rocks hidden beneath the surface of the water. As long as we stay between the boundaries he's recommended, nothing should go wrong."

Kat appeared unconvinced. "I . . . I'm having second thoughts," she said. "You know I don't do heights very well."

"I thought cats had nine lives," Bruce said. The pun drew a groan from the others.

Rosie took a step toward Kat. "Have you ever jumped into a pool from the high dive?"

"Yeah, once or twice. Maybe more."

"Well, then you'll do just fine. The bluff is only about twenty-five, maybe thirty feet high and it juts out over the water," Rosie said. "Hey, at that height it's actually more like a baby cliff. We're not talking the Grand Canyon here. It's really a lot of fun, trust me. Of course, you don't have to go—this is optional. But if you do, I'll be right there by your side."

Heather said, "Yeah, and don't forget she's had just a tiny bit of experience as an Olympic swimmer." She gave Kat a reassuring pat on the back.

"Any other questions?" Rosie said.

Bruce held up his towel and asked, "Could you refresh my memory—how do you make a tourniquet in the event of a shark bite?"

"BRUCE!" Heather and Jodi tried to push him overboard.

3:34 P.M.
Huntingdon Valley, Pennsylvania

"Mrs. Schultz, it's John Crans."

"I was hoping it was you," Amy said, pacing the kitchen floor, the cordless phone jammed against her ear. "Any progress?"

"Yes—and no. I've checked the master calendar and the school has several trips taking place over spring break."

"Really?"

"Let's see, the senior class took a trip to the Pocono Mountains—well, about 140 of the 642 in that class. It's sort of a traditional last hurrah not officially sponsored by the school."

"Justin is a junior."

"True. But it's possible he may have tagged along with an upper-

80

classman. That's frowned on, but it sometimes happens. Can't rule out the possibility he's there."

"I see."

"The tennis team with fourteen students is in a tournament in Pittsburgh. Both junior and seniors are involved."

"I don't believe Justin plays tennis."

"Uh-huh. Well, then there's the social studies class with a small group of juniors out on a houseboat in the Chesapeake Bay for the week. Looks like eight students plus the teacher and her husband," he said.

"Why don't—" She began to offer a suggestion.

"Excuse me, there's one more trip. The marching band is in Canada with 257 students at an international band competition. So, as you can see, Mrs. Schultz, with this much activity, things get very complicated."

"How so?"

"While I know the general details surrounding these trips, I don't have a specific list of students who are participating in each event. That is handled by the responsible teacher or coordinator. In each instance I've been working to reach the key contact by phone all afternoon," he said.

"Sounds like two or three phone calls and we'd have our answer, then, right?" For an instant Amy was hopeful.

"Actually, it's not as easy as all that. For starters, the houseboat doesn't have a phone and the teacher's phone must not be turned on, or perhaps they're out of range. We are trying to find out which company rented the boat because they'd know how to reach the boat by radio. Then . . ." John paused. "According to the schedule left with me by the band director, the marching band is in the middle of their competition, which runs well into the evening. Either the teacher can't hear his cell phone above the noise, or he's out of range. We're having the same trouble in the Poconos since the cabins don't have phones and there's no cell coverage in the mountains."

Amy could tell by his tone that Mr. Crans had invested more time than he had to spare. Was this just a wild-goose chase? Should she involve the police? Was there another way?

"There is one bright spot. I spoke with the tennis team coach, and he assured me Justin wasn't part of their group." He waited for a reply.

"Mrs. Schultz?"

"I'm still here. I just . . ." she hesitated, "I don't know what to do. I feel so helpless and I'm . . . I'm afraid something awful is going to happen if we don't find Justin—"

"I fully understand and, trust me, the student's safety is my top priority. But I've done everything I can so far. Now, all I've got to do is wait for a callback. I left a voice mail on the two cell phones explaining the urgency of the situation. So we wait and see. Not fun, is it?"

"Not in the least."

3:46 P.M.

"What a rush!" Stan shouted at the top of his lungs. He sprinted up the hillside to the top of the bluff. He had taken his third jump after spending part of the afternoon with Phil and Justin working on the anchor in the hull of the ship. He caught up with Kat, Jodi, Carlos, and Bruce. Rosie, who had just finished another dive, was down below swimming back to shore.

"What a total riot," Stan said, slightly out of breath. "I didn't know this was gonna be such a kick." He observed Jodi looking in the direction of his muscular chest. He flexed. "Nice, ain't it?"

Her eyes met his. "I was looking at the cross you're wearing—if you must know."

He grabbed his abs pretending to be stung by her comment.

She softened. "So why do you wear a cross, anyway?"

He reached for it. "I'm not really sure. Just thought it looked cool."

Stan could tell she wasn't buying his explanation.

"Okay, so it's kind of my good-luck charm. I kiss it before every football game. Got it from my mom for protection on the field. There. Are you happy?"

"I liked your first idea better."

They traded smirks.

"Hey, guys, speaking of ideas, why don't we try diving off that edge of the bluff?" Stan pointed past the scrub brush. "Look how soft the edge is. It's covered by moss. Probably won't be so tough on our feet."

Jodi looked skeptical. "I don't think that's such a good idea. Mrs. Meyer said we're supposed to stay between the pine tree and the scrub brush. Didn't you hear her?"

"No. I've been with Phil, remember? What does she know about cliff diving anyway?"

Jodi stared at him. "Stan, if you had been there, you'd know she was just telling us what Phil said."

"Did you actually hear him *say* don't dive over there?"

"Well, not exactly. But Mrs. Meyer—" Jodi started to explain.

Carlos cut in. "Jodi, since when do you believe what Mrs. Meyer says, anyway? I'm with Stan. He's right. My feet are getting kinda roughed up from these stones."

Stan looked at Bruce and Kat.

"Come on, you guys. Live a little. Just look at the water over there; it's even calmer than this spot," Stan said as he took a few steps toward the landing past the brush.

Bruce said to Kat, "You know, that part of the bluff doesn't look as high as it is here. Maybe we should give it a try."

Kat shrugged her shoulders. "I'm in."

"You guys go right ahead. I'm staying put," Jodi said, standing her ground. She looked after them as they trotted off. "What am I supposed to tell Mrs. Meyer?" she shouted, cupping her hands to her mouth.

Stan looked past Jodi and saw Mrs. Meyer in the distance just beginning to climb the hill. "If we hurry, she'll never know," Stan said then urged them to move faster.

Stan, Carlos, Bruce, and Kat had sprinted to the far side of the brush. Kat surveyed the view, but something troubled her. "Guys, I . . . I hate to say, but I've got a bad feeling about this." She crossed her arms.

"Oh, come on, Kat. I'll go first just to show you there's nothing to worry about." Stan took a position a few feet back from the edge. A moment later, he broke into a full-throttle run and shouted, "Geronimo!" He sailed into the air. Within seconds, he hit the water below and disappeared.

They looked down at the spot where he vanished.

An instant later, Stan burst through the surface of the water with a wide smile. "See, no problem!"

Carlos looked over his shoulder to Jodi, who remained fixed between the pine tree and scrub brush, and sneered. He turned to face the water, walked to the edge of the cliff, and launched into a cannonball.

After Stan and Carlos were swimming toward the shore, Bruce said to Kat, "Ladies first." He gave her a playful bow.

Kat took several tentative steps forward. Her heart started to pound. *All I have to do is take a baby step*, she thought, remembering a scene from *What about Bob?* Although she had jumped several times that afternoon from the approved site, the height still bothered her. Yet she had to admit this was fun. Like Stan, she was having a blast. She inched forward. Her toes felt the soft, moist moss-covered rock as she reached the edge.

She paused to scan the bay and found its unmistakable beauty enchanting. A slight updraft of warm air following the face of the bluff enveloped her. For an instant, she felt as if she could fly. She lingered, feeling at one with nature.

"You gonna jump, or do I need to push you?" Bruce teased from a few feet behind her.

"I'm going, I'm going . . . chill out."

Unlike the others, Kat didn't plan to attempt anything fancy — no cannonballs, no banana splits or can openers. Just a basic push off and jump, much like falling in a straitjacket. She was no pro, but she could swim. She just figured a basic jump was the best way to avoid a belly flop. Kat stood at the edge, crossed her fingers, and started to throw her arms back to propel herself forward when, without warning, she heard an angry shout: "*DON'T!*"

But Kat's body was already engaged and couldn't be stopped. On reflex, she snapped her neck around toward the source of the alarm behind her. Out of the corner of her eye Kat saw Mrs. Meyer running full steam in her direction.

Or was she running toward Bruce? Why would Mrs. Meyer do that?

Her immediate impulse was to attempt to pull back midjump, but gravity, like a massive magnet pulling her downward, worked against her efforts. She clawed at the air as if the emptiness would somehow prevent her fall. Kat's abrupt reversal caused her to lose her balance, her feet slipped out from under her on the wet mossy surface. She lost control.

In a jerky motion, like a puppet in the hands of an unskilled puppeteer, Kat's lower back slammed against the jagged jawlike edge of the massive rock. The harsh impact knocked the air out of her lungs and sent her tumbling into a full, helpless free fall. A fiery blast of pain shot through her twisting torso. While suspended between earth and sky, she cried out, "Oh, God!"

She blacked out before she plunged into the water below.

4:21 P.M.

Rosie dragged the little boat from its mooring on the shore. Her heart was pumping as if she just finished a swim meet. She had to get to Phil. He'd know how to contact the Coast Guard from the houseboat's radio.

As she hauled the boat back into the water, she glanced over her shoulder to see how Bruce was doing with Kat. Rosie was thankful Bruce knew CPR. At the moment he was attempting to revive Kat's near-lifeless body. From Rosie's position, it was difficult to know if he was making progress.

In her haste to climb in, Rosie slipped and cut her right leg on a corroded edge of the boat. Warm blood oozed from the gash. She winced, but didn't have time to worry about a minor scrape—not with Kat lying comatose on the beach.

After several sharp tugs on the pull cord, the engine sprang to life. Rosie adjusted the throttle and accelerated toward the houseboat anchored a hundred yards offshore. Even though she pushed the engine to the max, it felt as if her heart was racing faster than the boat.

In what felt like an eternity, Rosie pulled alongside the houseboat and began to yell for Phil as she secured the dinghy.

Phil stepped out onto the rear deck. "What's wrong?" She took his hand as he pulled her up onto the houseboat. She saw his face braced with intensity, especially as he glanced at the blood on her leg. "You're bleeding. What happened?"

She knew her husband's style. He'd want just the skinny. Rosie spat the information out. "Don't worry about me. There's been an accident. Kat's hurt pretty badly. She slipped on the cliff before a dive. Bruce is giving her CPR."

"Any visible wounds?"

"None that we could see. We checked before carrying her to shore. Bruce thinks there's a strong possibility of internal bleeding, but that's only a guess based on the way her back hit the cliff's edge."

Rosie watched his eyes narrow as his jaw muscles pulsated. She knew he was processing the information.

"Get the first aid kit, your purse, your cell phone, and grab a blanket. I'll radio our position and situation to the Coast Guard. We've got to stabilize her body temperature. We leave here in three minutes—sooner if possible."

4:29 P.M.
Fisherman's Wharf, Chesapeake Bay, Maryland

"Hello, Mr. Crans?"

"Speaking."

"Yeah, uh . . . John Crans? It's Joey at Bay Rentals. You the principal over there?"

"Yes. How can I help you?"

"Uh, according to my paperwork, we rented your school a houseboat for the week . . ."

"Excellent! We've been trying to find out which company rented the boat to our social studies teacher. I'm so glad you called."

"Maybe so. Maybe no. You haven't heard my news yet," Joey said.

John sat up straight in his chair. "What news?"

"See, I was just radioing all of our boat rentals to make sure they knew about the storm which is heading our way, probably hits tomorrow, you know. Should be lots of thunder, lightning, high winds—the works. These things are so hard to predict. Anyway, like I said, when I radioed the boat rented to your school, this guy Phil-somebody answered."

"Phil Meyer."

"Sure, sure. That's the guy. Kinda direct, if ya know what I mean. I didn't say more than a few words before he barked at me to keep the frequency clear. I wouldn't say he was real nasty-like. Just seemed, I don't know, rude, sorta—"

"That's it? You're calling to tell me Mr. Meyer was abrupt with you?" John asked, irritated.

"Well, no, not really—I mean, I'm all for free speech, but he did seem a bit over the top," Joey said.

John listened, waiting for the point of the conversation.

Joey continued. "Okay, like, when I sensed he was so mad, I asked him if there was some kinda problem. Get this. He says to me there's been an accident and, um, somebody got hurt . . . oh, and the Coast Guard was on the way."

John pressed the phone to his ear as he scribbled a quick note. "Did he say who got hurt . . . or anything else?"

"Sure, sure. He told me to go visit hell and to get off the radio— only not as nice as I just told you. Oh, and no, he didn't say who was injured. I figured you might oughta know."

"Great," John sighed. He began to massage his temples.

"Just doin' my job."

"No, I mean . . . oh, never mind. Do me a favor, will you?"

"Like what?"

"Two things. Maybe wait an hour or so then radio back to the boat and find out exactly what happened. I need details. I'll give you my home and cell phone numbers. Call me the instant you know more," John said then added, "please?"

"And the second thing?" Joey asked.

"This is very important. I need you to find out if one of the students on board is a Justin Moore. Got it?"

"Justin Moore. Sure, sure."

4:57 P.M.

Within twenty-four minutes, two Coast Guard emergency medevac team members in a helicopter touched down on the beach, carefully strapped Kat to a stretcher, hooked her up to an IV, and placed her on the chopper. As they worked, Rosie wanted to help, but knew she needed to let the pros handle things. Kat was still breathing, and that's what mattered most.

Now that the helicopter was ready to leave, Rosie attempted to climb in next to Kat. She was stopped by one of the Coast Guards.

"I'm coming with her," Rosie said in protest.

"Sorry, ma'am. I can't let you on board," he shouted above the noise from the overhead propeller.

Rosie was outraged. "I've got to go! She's my student. I'm responsible for her." She tried another approach. "I've got her parents' emergency release form in my bag." She tapped her purse as she spoke.

"Just give that to me," he yelled, his hand outstretched. "Hurry. We're wasting precious time!"

Rosie clutched her purse, then turned in the direction of Phil, who had been directing Bruce, Jodi, Stan, and Carlos into the motorboat. "*Phil!*"

He whirled around and raced to her side.

"Tell them that I need to go with Kat." Rosie looked at him in earnest.

Phil shot the Guard an icy glare. "What's the problem? You heard the lady. She's gotta go with you."

"Can't take her, sir. We'll be too heavy."

Phil swore. "I've flown those Dolphin choppers all around the world, and I know they're rated for six passengers—easy. That child needs her. She goes. Or do I need to radio your supervisor?" Phil stared him down.

Rosie watched the Guard lock eyes with Phil. She knew Phil wouldn't back down.

After a tense moment, the Guard said, "Give me your arm, ma'am."

6:53 P.M.

Jodi sat on the edge of Kat's bunk. Her feet touched the dusty floor-boards where Kat's clothing lay in a rumpled pile. While the others finished a light dinner in the gathering room, Jodi wanted to be alone. She couldn't imagine eating at a time like this. Not now, anyway.

This was all my fault, Jodi thought. *I should've insisted the others follow the rules. But how? What else could I have said? If I hadn't caved, maybe they would have listened to me and Kat wouldn't be hurt or dead.*

Several hours had passed since Kat was flown to the hospital, and they hadn't received any word on her status. Bruce suggested no news was good news. But that provided Jodi little comfort. Instead, she folded her hands in her lap as if to pray, but the words didn't come.

How long had she known Kat? Two days, maybe three. She was a total stranger. And yet, not really. Sure, Kat's lifestyle was wild and her clothes were as provocative as her interest in the Wiccan weird-ness. Still, Kat had something in common with Jodi: she was cre-ated in the image of God.

Jodi reached down and picked up Kat's jeans, socks, and tank top. As she began to carefully fold them, her thoughts shifted to Stan.

Poor Stan. After the helicopter was airborne, they had returned to the houseboat. Once back on board, Phil cross-examined each of them about the events leading up to the crisis. When Phil learned Stan urged the others to ignore the directions, Phil was enraged. He gave Stan a verbal thrashing like nothing she'd ever heard in her life. The exchange still echoed in Jodi's mind.

"Who do you think you are to disregard my rules?"

She remembered the dopey look on Stan's face. "I didn't think that—"

"Exactly. You didn't *think*. That's your problem. You don't know how to follow orders, do you? DO YOU?" Phil blasted away with both barrels.

Stan had shrugged his sagging shoulders then tried to look away. "I thought I had the right to do whatever I wanted so long as I wasn't hurting anyone. Besides, Kat didn't have to do what I did." Stan muttered.

Jodi guessed Phil was within an inch of Stan's face when he spat his next question. "What gave you the right to jeopardize the lives of others by your reckless *example?* What if Kat dies? How will you live with yourself then? And what if more than one person was wounded? Let me guess, you didn't think about that, either?"

Stan had cowered. Although he certainly deserved the rebuke, Jodi took no comfort in the thought that Stan da man must have soiled his pants as Phil had read him the riot act.

She stacked Kat's folded clothing at the end of the bed then began to talk with God.

"Lord, I pray for Kat wherever she is," she whispered the words out loud. "Please be with her and guide the doctors—help them find out what's wrong with her . . . forgive me for not taking more of a stand . . . and you know how just yesterday I was so rude to Kat. Forgive me for what I said to her. I . . . ." She stopped for a moment as a new series of thoughts flooded her mind.

What should she do now? Should she ask for the strength to pray for Kat with the other students? What would they think? Would they be uncomfortable at the suggestion? Would she be intolerant to bring religion into things? Or would they appreciate her sincerity? Then again, what sense would that make to the others since Kat was leaning toward witchcraft? Wouldn't the world be better off without her?

Jodi marveled at her own immature logic. *What kind of Christian am I to even hesitate to pray for Kat?* she wondered. She pushed the negative thoughts from her mind then continued to pray. "Lord, you love Kat as much as you love me. You died for her too. Help me to be more Christlike with Kat. And honestly, I'm scared. I need the strength and the words to pray for Kat with the group—at the right time. In Jesus' name, I beg, amen."

No sooner had she finished than she heard a light knock at the doorway.

"Hey," Heather said. "The door was open and it looked like you were praying. Sorry to interrupt."

Jodi nodded. "I was. What's up?"

"I've been thinking about what you said."

Jodi tilted her head as she waited for Heather to continue at her own pace.

"Well, I mean, what you said earlier today. I feel like I've been kinda coasting along in my faith, ya know?"

"Like how?"

"Ever since school started this year I've been sorta cold toward God. I really don't have a quiet time and I even forget to thank God before meals most of the time." Heather bit her lower lip and then leaned against the cabin doorjamb. "Remember how fired up we were after the missions trip last summer?"

Jodi nodded. "Totally. We were ready to save the whole school. Even talked about starting a Bible study together before school, remember?"

"Yeah, but I kinda put the brakes on that idea . . . I don't even know why." Heather shrugged and ran her fingers through her hair. "Might have had something to do with being popular—like you said. All I know is this year has been pretty hard for me and I think it's time I, like, I don't know . . . maybe I should rededicate myself to the Lord."

With a wave of her hand, Jodi motioned for Heather to sit beside her on the bed. As Heather approached, Jodi glanced at her friend's face. She noticed Heather's eyes were filling with tears. Jodi asked, "Here? Now?"

"Would you mind?" Heather asked. She gently brushed the tears away with the back of her hand. "Pray with me?"

"In a heartbeat!"

Heather sat next to Jodi. They joined hands and bowed their heads. After a quiet minute Heather began to pray.

"Dear Jesus, um, I'm not really sure where to start . . . all I know is I'm a sinner who's been . . . saved by grace. Still, I haven't been the best Christian. I've taken my eyes off of you and, well, I've been more concerned about my stuff than being focused on you and what you want for my life . . . I'm sorry. Please forgive me for taking you for granted . . . and for all of the times I blew my witness or like . . . when I've been more concerned about being accepted by friends than doing what pleases you. Thanks for a friend like Jodi who's always honest and isn't afraid to get into my face . . . in Jesus' name, amen."

"Amen," Jodi said and then squeezed Heather's hand.

"Oh yikes!" Heather blurted out.

Jodi almost jumped out of her seat. "What gives?"

"I almost forgot. Phil just got word from the hospital on Kat's condition."

"How . . . how is she?" Jodi perked up, expectant.

"I don't know. He wants to tell all of us together—right now. You wanna come sit with me?"

"I'll be right there."

7:21 P.M.

Jodi slipped into the main cabin and took a seat next to Heather on the green sofa. She noticed Vanessa, Carlos, and Justin sat on the floor while Stan and Bruce leaned against the galley counter. Little was said. Everyone was focused on Phil, who had just entered the room carrying a box of Kleenex.

Phil grabbed a folding chair, situated it so he could see everyone, and then sat down. He placed the tissues on the kitchen table to his left. Jodi assumed he brought the Kleenex for them since he didn't appear to be teary eyed.

"The Coast Guard just radioed an update on Kat," Phil began. "Rosie says I don't mince words. I'll be the first to admit she's right about that. Never been one who could sugarcoat reality. I'm not sure what the value of glossing over the truth would be, anyway." Phil paused and scanned their faces.

Jodi leaned forward, hanging on to the implication. Was Kat in serious trouble? Was she paralyzed? Is that what Phil was trying to say? Or worse—was she already dead?

Phil continued as if he had read Jodi's thoughts. "Let me cut to the chase. The good news is that, although her condition is critical, Kat *is* alive . . ."

Heather blurted out, "That's wonderful!" Vanessa and Carlos exhaled a sigh of relief. Stan and Bruce gave each other a high-five. Jodi remained focused.

"So what's the bad news?" Jodi asked, her eyes riveted on Phil.

Phil turned to Jodi. "I'm not a religious person, but unless God or whoever works a small miracle, at most she's got one week to live." His words hung like a thick cloud in the air above them.

Jodi's eyes moistened as she returned his gaze.

"Was it internal bleeding?" Bruce asked after a long silence.

"Yes, and worse," Phil said. "According to the doctor, both kidneys were so damaged by the fall that her left kidney failed. In fact, they've already removed it. Her right kidney isn't predicted to function more than three or four days."

"Are they *sure* everything is really that bad?" Heather asked.

"Kat might die? Come on, surely she'll be all right," Vanessa pleaded.

"I'm sorry, it doesn't look good," Phil said.

Jodi could feel the mood of the others in the room turning dark. Her own heart ached as she pictured Kat lying stretched out on the operating table, helpless, surrounded by doctors and nurses in sterilized, pale green scrubs.

"I had a feeling—I mean, the way she slammed her back against the rocks—something like that might happen," Bruce said, shaking his head.

Phil put a hand to his mouth as he cleared his throat. "There's more. Kat lost a lot of blood when they removed the left kidney. She needs more blood immediately. And, like I said, if she's gonna live, she'll need that new kidney within a few days."

Vanessa asked, "Which hospital is she at?"

"Abington."

"Well, at least that's a plus, right? Abington is one of the biggest hospitals around—" Vanessa stopped as Phil held up his hand.

"Turns out Kat's blood type is AB-negative. That presents a problem in several ways. First, Abington has a severe shortage of AB-negative—in fact, their supplies are virtually depleted."

Carlos looked indignant. "How could they let that happen? What kind of idiots are running the place?"

"Actually, Carlos," Phil said evenly, "Abington is in short supply thanks in part to the strict requirements for screening blood these days. The risk of obtaining blood contaminated with the HIV virus and passing it on to another patient is very real." Phil paused and leaned forward in his chair and folded his hands together.

"I'm not here to lecture. My wife's the teacher in the family. But, frankly, when people do risky things with their behavior, they promote the spread of diseased blood. Seems this is a real consequence of what I overheard you say was someone's 'private sexual choice.'"

"You heard me say that?"

"I don't miss much."

Carlos started to respond then stopped.

Phil continued. "The second problem is that due to Kat's blood composition, it would be a rare person who could provide a donor organ match. He or she would have to be AB-negative and in good health—not to mention willing and available immediately for the transplant."

Heather reached for the Kleenex to dry her tears.

Phil handed her the box. "Like I said, I don't know how to sugar-coat things. I'm sorry for your friend. I'm even more sorry that this whole incident could have been prevented." He didn't look at Stan. Everyone understood Phil's message.

Jodi stole a look in Stan's direction. His gaze was fixed on a spot on the floor.

Without looking up, Stan said, "If you'll excuse me, I got to use the john." With that he turned and left.

Bruce stepped out of Stan's way then asked, "I know compared to Kat's situation this isn't important . . . but what happens to the rest of our trip?"

Several nodded, sharing the same concern.

Jodi noticed Phil had anticipated the question. "Tomorrow after breakfast, we've got to head home. Under normal conditions it would take about half of a day to reach Fisherman's Wharf. This tug's top speed is just over six knots. Based upon our current position, that puts us dockside on Wednesday, early afternoon."

"What do you mean by normal conditions?" Carlos asked.

"When the Coast Guard radioed, they also provided an update on the storm we've been tracking. It's heading inland from the east. They estimate it should hit us by late morning tomorrow," Phil said. "And the winds are stronger than first estimated. It's gonna be rough sailing."

"Oh, that's just great," Carlos said. "Can't we leave right now and get a jump on the storm?"

"No. It's too dangerous to travel in the dark. We'll pull up anchor at first light."

Jodi couldn't help but notice the sea of worried expressions.

She guessed Phil must have had the same impression when he added, "My responsibility is to get us all back to land without further problems. And I intend to do so. You can bank on that."

Jodi squirmed in her seat as she listened to Phil give Kat's medical report. She hated hospitals. The whole medical scene rattled her nerves ever since she watched her grandfather die a slow, painful death from cancer several years ago. The injections. The chemotherapy. The loss of his hair, weight, and bodily functions. She could almost smell the dreadful antiseptic scent as she imagined Kat, like her grandfather, confined in that institution.

But something else gnawed at Jodi: she knew her blood type was also AB-negative.

The whole time Phil spoke, she knew she could give up a kidney so Kat could live. Without it, according to Phil, Kat would die. But what was the right thing to do? *Was* there a right thing to do? All week long Jodi had been told that concepts of right and wrong were outdated.

According to Mrs. Meyer's view of the world, Jodi would be under no moral obligation to save the life of another. It's survival of the fittest, right? Every man for himself. Just mind your own business and do what works best for you—that's your truth.

Jodi fidgeted with a loose thread on the sofa's armrest. After some hesitation, Jodi decided to share her dilemma.

"Excuse me, everyone, but, um, I could use your help with a tough decision," Jodi said. They all looked in her direction. She turned to Heather and added, "Better pass me a couple of those tissues just in case."

"Here ya go," Heather said, sharing the box.

Jodi thanked her, pulled out a tissue, and clutched it for moral support.

"Where to start?" Jodi asked herself under her breath. She

paused to arrange her thoughts. "Okay. Assume for a minute you and Kat have the same blood type. Would any of you be willing to donate your own blood to help Kat?"

The group was quick to respond.

"Are you kidding? I'd do it in a heartbeat," Heather said.

"For a sister, you know it, girl," Vanessa said.

"So would I," Bruce said, adding, "no question."

Even Justin nodded and gave a thumbs-up.

Jodi wasn't surprised by the unanimous opinion that they'd all be glad to give blood. She waited until everyone was finished then asked, "But why?"

Carlos tossed her a look of disbelief. "What kind of dumb question is that? To save her life, of course."

"Because it would be the right thing to do," Vanessa said.

"And life is valuable," said Heather.

Bruce nodded. "Gotta heed the need."

"Now, let me ask you this," Jodi said. "Assume once again you and Kat have the same blood type. Would you donate the kidney she needs?"

Several were about to respond. Jodi held up her hand and waved them off. "Before you answer, consider this: If you're the donor, you gotta understand you can't live without at least one working kidney. If for some reason your last kidney got damaged, I don't know, like by trauma from a car accident, an infection, or disease, you'd face a life of dialysis or you might even be looking for a transplant yourself. With that in mind, what would you do?"

Jodi watched the discomfort around the room. Vanessa sat on her hands. Bruce looked down at his feet. Justin rocked in place. Carlos folded his arms. Heather crossed her legs.

No one spoke.

"Just a minute ago we said we'd give blood to save her life, that life was valuable, that we'd be doing the right thing," Jodi said. "So why the hesitation now?"

Carlos shook his head. "Jodi, what kind of game is this? Kat's dying in the hospital, and all you can do is make us feel guilty with this crazy hypothetical situation?"

"I don't think I could do it," Heather admitted.

"Neither would I," Vanessa confessed. "I mean, the thought of being a living donor—we're all so young and there's so much life ahead of us . . ."

Bruce looked up from the floor. "Just because none of us wants to make that sacrifice, what are you saying, Jodi? We're bad people?"

Jodi swallowed hard then started to cry, softly at first. She knew the others must be puzzled and embarrassed for her as she dabbed her moist eyes. "I'm sorry . . ." Jodi felt Heather's arm on her shoulder. "Guys, this is no game . . . and no, Carlos, it isn't a hypothetical situation."

Jodi struggled to hold back her tears. She cleared her throat before continuing. "Remember our first night together . . . by the campfire? I told you my blood type is AB-negative *just like Kat's*. Don't you see? I can save her life if I give her one of my kidneys. That's my dilemma," she said as she studied the stunned faces in the room.

Nobody moved, except for Stan who returned from the bathroom. He stood next to Bruce. "What'd I miss?"

Jodi ignored his question and reached for another tissue. Once she regained her composure, she said to the group, "This isn't a fire drill—it's the real thing, ya know? The time for me to act is now and I . . . I just don't know what to do. Me of all people . . . I agree life is precious because God created it that way. But I'm only human. Why should I sacrifice? What's in it for me? I'd like to know why, when it's not even in my best interest, should I take the risk? Would it be wrong for me to just say, 'Too bad, Kat'?"

Again, silence. She could tell the others didn't know what to say. After a long minute, she turned toward Phil and asked, "What do you think Mrs. Meyer would say I should do?"

Phil scratched his head. "I, well . . . I don't really know how she'd respond."

Jodi could tell Phil was in an awkward spot.

He leaned forward. "Now if you were to ask me . . ."

"Please. I'd like to know."

"Well, in the military we had a saying: 'Never leave a man behind.' You'd risk your own life to rescue a wounded soldier in the field. Didn't matter if you liked him or not. Didn't matter if it was convenient. Didn't matter if you thought he'd make it. If he shared your uniform, you'd put your life on the line to save his."

"I see," Jodi said, her voice unsteady.

Heather reached over and squeezed Jodi's hand. "Whatcha going to do, sis?"

Jodi looked at her through teary eyes. "I just don't know."

9:30 P.M.
Huntingdon Valley, Pennsylvania

All afternoon, Amy Schultz's spirit was troubled. Where was Justin? Was he okay—or was he mixed up in some kind of mischief? Why hadn't John Crans called with something, anything? Was it really that hard to contact the teachers in charge of those school trips? Surely the school must have made some contact with them by now.

Amy couldn't shake the nagging feeling that Justin was up to something—precisely what, she didn't know. She was familiar with the parade of news stories about kids who planned violent crimes in school—and the parents who didn't know or didn't bother to check their kids' bedrooms where a complete arsenal of bombs, guns, and knifes were being stashed.

His room, she thought. *I haven't even looked for signs he might be angry enough to carry out . . .*

Would he actually do something like that?

How well did she know him, anyway?

Her thoughts propelled her down the hall to Justin's room. His door was ajar. She pushed it open, and then stepped in. She looked under his bed and in the closet. She opened his dresser drawers and scanned the contents.

As she worked, she knew they didn't have any guns in the house, aside from a little BB gun her husband used as a kid to shoot cans. She continued her search. Finding nothing, she thought, *Maybe he stole a gun . . . or a knife . . .*

A knife! She had to be sure. She went to the kitchen and counted the knives. None were missing.

Satisfied Justin wasn't stockpiling weapons, Amy had to do something with her nervous energy. She washed and folded the dirty clothes, vacuumed the house, emptied the trash cans throughout their modest ranch-style home, even dusted the mini-blinds. She didn't watch any TV; she couldn't bear the thought of sitting still— at least not until she got some word from the school about Justin.

She pulled a batch of chocolate-chip cookies from the oven. Baking cookies for her husband was all she could think of doing to pass the rest of the time before trying to go to sleep. Her husband was already in bed catching up on some reading.

Amy arranged a few cookies on a plate, poured two glasses of milk, and joined Michael in the bedroom. The bedside phone purred. Startled, Amy put the tray down, shot a look at the clock, then at her husband. She snatched up the phone.

"Hello, it's Amy," she said as she sat on the bed.

"Hope I didn't call too late. It's John Crans."

Amy covered the mouthpiece and whispered to her husband, "It's the principal." She spoke into the phone. "No, no. We're still up. We're on pins and needles over here! Any news on Justin?" she asked, hopeful.

"Not precisely. Here's what I've been able to learn. I got a call back from the teacher in charge of the marching band. He assured me Justin was not with them."

"Well, that's good news, I mean, at least he isn't in Canada, right?" Amy tried to sound upbeat.

"True. As I said before, he's not with our tennis team in Pittsburgh. And, to the best of my knowledge, he didn't go with the seniors to the Pocono Mountains."

"How can you be sure?"

"I spoke with the bus company contracted to transport the students. Just our luck, they require a list of passengers to be filed with their office. I was under the impression the students drove themselves, but I learned this year they decided to take buses. Anyway, unless Justin drove on his own, I think it's safe to say he didn't make that trip."

"Justin doesn't have a car," Amy said, mentally crossing off that possibility. "What about the boat trip?"

"Well, we've run into a small problem with the houseboat."

"Problem? What do you mean by that?"

"Actually, it's too early to know what's really going on . . ."

She waited but sensed John was reluctant to say more.

"Mr. Crans, my husband and I have been worried sick all day about Justin. We'd be grateful to have at least some idea of what's going on." Amy bit her lip, hoping he'd provide the details.

"Listen, I don't want to alarm you. There's no evidence yet that Justin is on the houseboat," he began then stopped.

"So you've been able to contact the boat?"

"Yes and no." John paused. "Okay, here's the situation. Late this afternoon, I received a call from Bay Rentals, the company that rented the houseboat to Mrs. Meyer. She's the teacher in charge. I was told that there was some kind of accident involving one of the students."

Amy felt the hair on the back of her neck bristle. "What kind of accident? Who was hurt? Who's on board?" *Dear God*, she said under her breath.

"Like I said, we don't have much to work on . . ."

She was puzzled. "I thought you said the boat company was in touch with the houseboat?"

"True. But only briefly. The teacher's husband, Mr. Meyer, had to keep the radio clear so the Coast Guard could communicate with them about the emergency. Mr. Meyer terminated the contact before Bay Rentals could learn more. That's when I got their call. Bottom line, I explained to the company official how urgent it was for us to verify whether your son was on board. He promised to try again."

"And?"

"Just before I called you, I got another call from Bay Rentals. They have been trying for the past two hours to reach the houseboat by radio but they've been unable to get any response."

Amy considered that for a moment. "What could that mean? Is the boat out of range?"

"Unlikely. According to Bay Rentals, there are only two plausible reasons. First, the boat is unoccupied. That's doubtful since it's so late. The other option is that the radio went dead."

Amy was beside herself. "Dead? What would cause that?"

"I wish I knew."

10:43 P.M.

Jodi lay inside her sleeping bag on the top bunk. She closed her eyes for what seemed the hundredth time as she tried to fall asleep, but thoughts of Kat kept her awake. Jodi couldn't shake the picture of Kat as she lay on the beach, gasping for air. Or the image of her body strapped onto the stretcher. Or the way Kat managed to cough out the words "Pray for me" to Jodi as the Coast Guard carried her away.

A tear rolled down Jodi's cheek at the memory. She whispered, *"God, I can't handle this!"* She wished she were home.

Jodi covered her head with her pillow to muffle the sound of the wind. She felt the boat sway more than usual. Phil had warned them to expect the stormy weather, beginning with higher-than-average winds overnight. Intense thunder and rain would follow at some point on Wednesday. At the moment, Jodi faced a very different kind of storm inside her mind.

If I give Kat a kidney, she thought, *I've got to face the hospital scene again . . . all those sick and dying people and the putrid sterile smell everywhere. And the needles—I hate getting stuck with a needle. Half the time they miss my vein and have to stick me again . . . Besides, will I still be able to live a full life with just one kidney? Can I do all the things I've done before? Can I travel to debates? Can I swim? Would a man still want me one day if he saw a huge scar on my side? Will I be able to chase the things I've always dreamed of doing?*

"And Jesus," she mouthed the words, "why do I always have to be the good girl who does the right thing? Am I being selfish to wish I wasn't here facing this decision? I mean, this is gonna cost me big time . . . It isn't volunteering to serve Thanksgiving dinner at the mission or donating time in the church nursery. We're talking cutting me open to give away a vital organ. Are you really asking me to make this sacrifice? Can't you get somebody else to do it? Someone older who's gonna die anyway . . . or maybe just someone who can handle it."

In the silence that followed, the words of Jesus in John 15, one of her favorite passages, came to mind: "Greater love has no one than this, than to lay down one's life for his friends."

She yanked the pillow off of her face and stared at the darkness. "Yeah, but she wasn't my friend!" Jodi said aloud then covered her face again with the pillow.

She had known Kat for such a short time. Sometimes that's all the time life dealt you, sometimes even less. What kind of impression had she made on Kat? Probably not the best. Would there be a second chance to be more loving? More Christlike? Maybe. Was this her chance?

She rolled on her side.

Several minutes passed. She still couldn't sleep.

It was then that she recalled the words from 1 John 4:20—words she had read on Sunday before Mrs. Meyer made her put her Bible away: "If someone says, 'I love God,' and hates his brother, he is a liar; for he who does not love his brother whom he has seen, how can he love God whom he has not seen?"

So this is what Jacob must have felt like when he wrestled with the angel of God, she thought.

She unzipped her sleeping bag and sat upright. The top of her head brushed against the low ceiling. "Jesus, you know I love you, don't you?" she asked softly. "Are you asking me to demonstrate your love to Kat by doing this? Is that what you're up to here? If this is you, I need you to just show me."

She folded her hands in her lap and waited. For what, she wasn't sure. Handwriting on the wall would have been helpful. Maybe a burning bush experience . . . or a visit from an angel. Would that be too much of a sign to ask for?

Instead, a strange, unexplainable peace swept over her. She felt a warmth in her spirit that both quieted her fears and answered her cry for direction.

That's it. God wants to reach Kat—and maybe some of the others—through my decision. I've always said that my life is not my own, so why am I surprised that God arranged for me to be in this place . . . for this purpose?

She'd take the step of faith. She'd trust that God's grace would be sufficient to sustain her. And she figured her parents would stand by her decision too, especially once they knew her kidney would provide Kat with a fighting chance to live.

Jodi would ask them to be sure.

"Okay, Jesus," she said, "you know I'm such a wimp when it

comes to hospitals and surgery. I'm counting on you to see me through this!"

With that, she took a deep breath, lay back down, and drifted into a smooth, peaceful sleep.

Wednesday

3:37 A.M.

The houseboat managed to maintain a comfortable cabin temperature, especially given its vintage. Never too warm, never too cool. Yet, tonight he was simultaneously too hot and too cold as he lay on the lower bunk. Beads of sweat formed on his forehead, while his body shivered to stay warm. Must be nerves.

He removed his wristwatch from his left forearm and pushed a button to activate the backlight on his watch: 3:37. It was now or never. The time had come for him to do what he came to do. He was ready, and the sound of his roommate's snoring was a good omen.

He used his abs to sit up, carefully lowered his feet onto the floor, and placed his watch on his pillow. His plan required him to act before daylight.

He had worn black sweatpants and a black sweatshirt to bed that night and placed his denim backpack next to the bed. He reached inside and wrapped his hand around the handle of the seven-inch dagger. With a smooth, steady motion, he withdrew the blade, and then stood, barefoot, to his full height. He didn't wear shoes for fear of the noise they might make.

Behind him, the heavy snoring was almost comical. He turned in the direction of the sound. Although he couldn't quite see, he figured his roommate's mouth must be wide open. If only he had a tape recorder to capture the snorts, gasps, and wheezing . . . then again, what would be the point of that now? He fought the urge to pinch his roommate's nose shut.

Never mind. He was wasting time. He turned to leave.

The moon's glow, as on other nights, furnished a meager supply of light. As a vampire fears daylight, he feared the exposure that light would bring. He welcomed the dark shadows and would use them to hide his actions.

When he faced the bedroom door, he stopped long enough to mentally rehearse his movements. Satisfied with the details of his game plan, he opened the door slowly, like a member of the bomb squad working to defuse an armed explosive.

He stepped into the hallway, the knife clutched in his right hand, and paused. His eyes were attracted to the small night-light plugged into an outlet at floor level. Its dim, yellowish two-watt bulb flickered, more from age than design. He reached down, unplugged it, and then laid it on the floor. Darkness was his friend.

He waited a long moment for his eyes to adjust to the faint moonlight reflecting off the surface of the water into the hall through a series of small, round windows. It did little to illuminate his path, but it would have to do. He dare not use his penlight even for a moment.

The three cabins on the main level were arranged like ducks, sitting in a straight row. Each of the sleeping quarters had a thin door that adjoined the narrow passageway. The hallway ran the length of the ship. It connected the galley and main cabin in the forward compartment to the deck on the back of the ship. His cabin was the closest to the galley. Phil's was the farthest.

He inched his door closed with his left hand, then turned toward the rear of the houseboat. Each step was slow, steady, and taken with purpose.

The hall floor was covered with a cheap, rubber-backed carpet that did little to muffle the sound of his movements. Even though he stepped lightly, he was grateful for the sound of the wind, which provided the perfect cover for his footsteps.

As he made his way down the hall, his left hand tested the middle cabin door. Good. It was shut tight. Just a few feet more. He stood outside of Phil's door. In the darkness he felt around the doorjamb and determined that it, too, was closed. The better to mask any sounds—until it would be too late, he thought.

He retraced his steps toward the galley. His forward motion was as slow as molasses on a cold day. He had to be careful. He couldn't afford to brush against the wall as the boat swayed from the force of the wind. He passed the middle cabin door.

A sudden creaking sound behind him caused him to stop cold in his tracks. His ears perked up. A door opening? The veins on the side of his neck throbbed from the rush of adrenaline. His grasp on the knife tightened.

There it was again. This time more pronounced. It appeared to originate overhead. He considered that for a minute. The two cabins for the girls were on the upper deck. Probably just someone tossing in their sleep.

He exhaled and remembered to breathe again.

When no other sound was detected, he took another step. Then another. Soon he reached the end of the hall, opened the door that led into the galley and gathering room, stepped in, and closed the door behind him.

Once inside, he withdrew his penlight and flicked it on to regain his bearings. He recalled that the room had three lamps. He had made a mental note of them during their daily sessions.

The first was located on the kitchen table. To his right, a floor lamp was parked in the far corner by the green sofa. And a third light was located above the sink in the kitchen. They were presently turned off.

He wanted them to stay that way.

One by one, he removed the bulbs and, careful not to make any more noise than was absolutely necessary, placed them in the trash. As he worked, something Jodi said in that very room yesterday, or was it the day before, echoed in his mind: "*Men love darkness rather than light.*"

How right you are, Jodi, he thought. *Especially now.* He depended on the cover of darkness to conceal his actions for as long as possible. If someone flipped on a light, that would complicate matters. He placed the last of the bulbs in the wastebasket then moved through the space to lower each of the window shades. He turned off his penlight.

At last, the room was devoid of light. Perfect.

He took a seat at the kitchen table and laid his knife on the cold Formica surface. From the pocket in his sweats he removed a single, folded sheet of paper and a pen. He placed them on the tabletop then unfolded the page without making a sound.

He leaned back in his chair.

As he sat in the blackness, he listened. He heard the waves slapping the side of the boat as if giving it a spanking, while the wind tossed some of the rigging against its mast. The mast, as Phil had been so kind to point out, supported the antenna for the ship's radio.

A mischievous smile formed on his lips. He knew the reason for the clanging. Earlier he had snipped about an inch out of the antenna feed, leaving the severed ends to dangle in the wind. The radio was dead. Phil almost caught him, but it was a chance he had to take.

No point having Phil contacting the Coast Guard for help.

3:44 A.M.
Huntingdon Valley, Pennsylvania

Amy Schultz woke with a jolt.

She glanced at the clock. Almost 4 A.M.

Unlike her husband, she wasn't a light sleeper. She could snooze through anything—thunder, lightning, barking dogs. Her childhood home backed up to a train track, so she learned to sleep through the rumble of the passing midnight freight train.

It was the rare occasion when she'd find herself staring at the ceiling in the middle of the night. But tonight, as she bolted upright, it felt as if God himself had nudged her awake. But why? It had to be Justin.

Amy knelt beside her bed to pray. She buried her face in her hands. Her lips moved, but she made no sound as the words flowed from her heart.

"Lord Jesus, for several days you know how I've carried this great weight . . . this burden for our son. But tonight I feel an intense heaviness in my spirit to pray for Justin . . . right now . . . and I don't know why, but you do . . ."

She pictured Justin's face.

"I know I haven't been the best mom; help me to love him better. He's been through so much pain in his life, so I commit him into your hands for safekeeping. You know where he is at this very moment. You know all the details of his circumstance, and you understand what his needs are. Please, I pray especially that you keep him from the evil one. Place a hedge of protection around him with your strong, mighty arms . . ."

Amy paused. Her thoughts were directed to the Scriptures—something she had just studied in her weekly Bible Study Fellowship meeting came to mind. She continued in prayer.

"You sent the prophet Elijah the raven with food during a

time of famine and persecution. In the same way, please provide Justin with all he stands in need of right now . . . whatever that may be, according to your mercy and grace. I know how much you love Justin. Thank you for hearing my prayer. In Jesus' name, amen."

Amy climbed back into bed and closed her eyes.

A moment later she opened them.

"Honey," she gently tapped her husband's shoulder.

"Hmm?"

"Babe, I think the Lord wants us to pray together for Justin."

"What?"

"Will you pray with me?"

"Now? I'm sleeping . . . or was . . ."

"Yes, now—more than ever."

3:51 A.M.

In a few minutes, he would begin. And just as quickly, he would be finished. Like a drowning man struggling to reach the surface for air, he was determined to make his move before the sun took its place in the sky.

In the dark, he reached for his penlight, clicked it on, and laid it on its side, arranging the beam so he could see his sheet of paper. He sat motionless as his eyes fixed on the page before him. Why was a note frequently involved in death? What prompted a person to leave one final calling card? Was it an unwritten contract with the rest of the human race to offer a rare glimpse into the reasons people acted the way they did?

Whatever the cause, he, like others before him, felt compelled to explain his actions. He picked up the pen and wrote with intensity. The palm of his hand was moist as he squeezed the pen and emptied his heart. It wouldn't be long now before his pain was paci-

THE MIND SIEGE PROJECT

fied. And yet, death was being impatient; it beckoned him to get on with it. His pen danced across the page.

As he wrote, a strange sensation came over him—a firmness of purpose mixed with a sense of dread. A fear of the unknown. An understanding that there was no way back. Oddly, he wondered how he would be remembered. As a coward? A person of principle or nothing more than a crazed maniac? He considered that for a moment and decided, no, it really didn't matter what people thought.

But something else bothered him. It was the way Jodi had offered to pray for Kat last night. What was it she had said? He pictured her as Jodi's words came back to him, *"You know, I believe in the power of prayer. Prayer changes things . . . Even when my problems in life appear hopeless, God is there and he cares."*

He shook his head in disagreement. Did God really care? Should he give prayer a try? Jodi had displayed the courage to pray. No. It was too late for prayer, he decided. He was convinced his solution was the right thing to do.

Then a new thought surfaced. If Mrs. Meyer were here, he wondered, would she agree with his course of action? Didn't she say, "Who's to say what's right?" Then again, maybe this time she'd say his choice was wrong. Whatever. At least this much could be said—it was his truth.

A few more words escaped his pen. This was his solution. This was the only way he knew to silence the voices. He regretted if some would feel it was a senseless act. After another minute he was finished. There. They'd know everything.

Without rereading the note, he scribbled his name at the bottom, placed his pen on the table, and reached for the penlight to switch it off. As he lifted the penlight, the narrow beam cast a ray of light on the door to the hallway.

It wasn't fully closed. A flicker of fear sparked inside of him.

He was certain he had pulled it shut. Didn't he? Maybe his mind was just playing tricks. He hadn't heard any sounds or movement—

aside from the waves and the gentle rain that fell with a soft patter on the boat's surface. Must have been an oversight. Then again, he remembered the time Phil entered the room during their first session. Phil had appeared, unexpected, almost out of thin air.

He switched off the penlight and slipped it into his pocket. In the blackness he lingered for thirty seconds, still perplexed by the opened door, before he reached for the knife. He picked it up; the handle felt cold to his touch. His heart began to beat wildly within his chest like African drums.

He knew the time had come to play his last card.

He was about to stand when, without warning, he found himself knocked to the floor, his legs still straddling the chair. His mind raced to catch up with the flood of sensations his nervous system reported . . . a blast of pain like a dozen needles jammed into a pincushion shot through the tissues on his left side . . . his head pounded where it banged against the flooring . . . his left leg, as if stung by a swarm of angry hornets, throbbed under the weight of the chair which pinned it to the floor. His heart battled against his rib cage.

He panicked. With a kick he struggled to rid himself of this unseen newcomer. The chair sailed across the room and collided into the wall. As he thrashed to break free, his knife accidentally grazed the side of his abdomen, splitting open his sweatshirt. He felt his blood, sticky and warm, begin to flow as the edge of the dagger sliced his skin. Like a wounded animal, he let out a hollow grunt. His breath came in heaves.

With what little control he managed over his limbs, he thrust himself against his opponent, slamming both of them into the leg of the table. The lamp crashed, sending shards of glass in every direction. The knife fell from his hand and slid out of reach in the darkness. Still clutching his wounded side, he managed to stand, his head dizzy and disoriented.

Who was this phantom? How did he know . . . where was he now? If only he could see . . .

His massive hands swatted at the blackness, hoping to make contact with the advance of this unknown person. With a smack, his right arm caught the stranger in the midsection, but rather than knocking him off balance, the outsider grabbed his arm and twisted it until fire, like a thousand darts, burned his body with a fresh wave of pain. His yell ripped the night air.

A gloved hand from the intruder reached around and sought to muzzle his mouth. He strained in vain to shake the unwelcome visitor off his back. In a last-ditch effort, he tossed his weight forward, which hurled them in the direction of the sofa. They struck the edge of the armrest then collapsed on the floor.

As he struggled, his forearm brushed against an object. The knife. He heard it slide and spin in place from the force of his bodily contact. If only he could grab it—without grabbing the wrong end. Suddenly he longed for just a flash of light, enough to see the position of the knife.

The penlight. He had tucked it into his pocket. His mind raced to consider his options. He'd have to shake this monkey off of his back long enough to retrieve the penlight—maybe a second or two, another second to flick it on, then an instant more to seize the blade. Three, maybe four seconds max.

That's all he'd need.

He clenched his teeth and snarled like a rabid dog, hunched his back, and shot forward. The unexpected burst of motion gave him the freedom from his assailant he needed. He snatched the penlight from his sweatpants, snapped it on, aimed it in the direction of the knife, and saw its position.

He dove for it. So did his nemesis.

The two bodies wrestled for control, entwined in a mortal combat that he felt he was rapidly losing.

3:54 A.M.

Jodi's cabin was directly above the galley. For several restless minutes, unbeknown to her, she tossed in her sleeping bag as her subconscious mind attempted to process the unsettling noises below. It was the yell that yanked her out of her dreams into a harsh reality.

Jodi sat upright with a shot. She was suddenly wide-eyed yet remained in a state of confusion. What in the world was going on below? Another prank? How could they? Certainly not at a time like this—with Kat in the hospital.

She strained to hear what was going on, but the rain that fell, heavier now, on the flimsy roof surface just above her head drowned out most of the sound. She'd put her ear to the door for a better listen.

She grabbed her flashlight from a small shelf on the wall next to her bunk but decided against using it at the moment. She unzipped her sleeping bag, swung her legs over the edge of the bed, and forgetting she was on the top bunk, took a step. She hit the floor with a thud.

"What a dork," she said aloud, embarrassed by her carelessness.

As she stood, Jodi's head banged against the bottom edge of the upper bunk. She winced and dropped her flashlight. She reached around to the back of her head and rubbed the spot where a slight abrasion had appeared. She knelt down to search for her flashlight.

Ten seconds later, upon finding it, she stood, this time with more care, then switched it on.

The battery, she observed, was weak at best. She tapped it in her left palm. For an instant the light strengthened then dimmed. With it, she spotted her slippers, slid her feet in, and then shuffled toward her door. She paused and listened to the dull, thudding noises on the first level.

Jodi cracked the door open.

It was one of those moments when a small voice from some corner of her mind warned her to lock the door and stay out of the way. Her fear, like cement boots, kept her from taking another step. And yet, her curiosity pressured her to make sense out of the situation.

Maybe it's Justin stumbling around in the dark, she thought. She recalled their first night around the campfire trading secrets when he revealed he was a sleepwalker. Jodi felt her heartbeat quicken. She wasn't about to go back to sleep. What harm could there be in finding out?

She stepped into the hall and aimed the feeble ray from her flashlight in the direction of the spiral staircase, which connected the upper and lower floors. The steps led to a corner in the main cabin. That's odd, she thought. As far as she could make out, there wasn't any light downstairs where the hostile noises, now more pronounced, appeared to originate.

Like a moth to a flame, Jodi was drawn to the activity below. She tiptoed closer. Her flashlight struggled to remain lit.

At the top of the narrow, aluminum stairs, she gripped the handrail and took three steps downward. A cacophony of grunts, groans, and thuds soared up the stairway. She froze on the third step.

It was then that her flashlight died.

"Oh, great. Now what?" Jodi thought, her feet riveted to the steps. Her flashlight was as useless as notes at a debate. Worse, she didn't have any spare batteries back in her bedroom.

Should she call out to the person below? Should she follow the spiral steps down and turn on the lamp on the kitchen table? Or should she turn and run as fast as she could back to the safety of her room? Or better, go wake up Heather and Vanessa? She turned to go get the other girls then, on second thought, stopped. *What if someone is hurt? Maybe I can help.*

As she took a step downward, a voice cried out in the darkness, "Let go—I'm bleeding!"

She covered her mouth and choked back a scream. Her knees felt as if they were about to buckle as her mind raced. This was no practical joke. This wasn't a case of sleepwalking. Something monstrous was unfolding, and she had to alert Phil. But how? This was the only way down. Should she chance it? Should she yell for help? Could Phil even hear her?

Jodi remained frozen in place, fearful of what she might get mixed up in if discovered.

Another series of sounds, like machine gun fire, shattered the thick air. Whoever—whatever—as down there collided with a chair, she guessed. Then, with a crash, she heard what must have been the hall door bursting open. A fast second later, she saw a flash of light then a yell. Was that Bruce?

Jodi's mind couldn't sort out the sensations. And where was Phil? She *had* to get to Phil.

No sooner had the thought crossed her mind than Phil's voice boomed into the room.

"HOLD IT RIGHT THERE! DON'T MOVE A MUSCLE!"

Jodi could see Phil standing in the doorway with a powerful flashlight trained in the direction of the table below, though she couldn't quite make out his target for herself. Not, at least, from her current position. Jodi's anxiety eased enough for her to take several quick steps down the spiral staircase for a better view.

At first glimpse Jodi almost didn't recognize the panic-stricken Bruce pressed up against the galley counter.

Toward the center of the room Jodi saw two figures dressed in black; somebody was stretched out on the floor. The second person had his knee rammed into the lower back of the guy on the floor.

Wait a minute, she thought, *that's Justin. He's got Stan pinned facedown on the floor . . . and he's holding a knife over Stan's body. What in the world? . . . Oh, dear Jesus, Stan is bleeding . . .*

Jodi, who was halfway down the stairs, shrieked. She instinctively turned to run upstairs to the safety of her cabin when she found her pathway blocked by Heather and Vanessa, who looked as if they had just awakened.

Phil barked out another order. "Stop right there. Not another step."

Jodi jerked her head around. Although she could tell he hadn't taken his eyes off of Justin and Stan, she knew Phil had directed his order at them. She was too scared to do anything but comply. Behind her, Heather and Vanessa started to weep.

"Oh God! Oh *God!*" Vanessa muttered through her tears.

Phil's voice rumbled. "Girls, knock it off."

They covered their mouths.

Jodi's eyes darted from Phil to the boys. In one hand, Phil trained his flashlight at the two boys; in the other hand, he aimed his 9 mm pistol in the direction of Justin's head.

Stan used the momentary distraction to try, in vain, to break free. Justin's hold, like a vise grip, couldn't easily be shaken.

Phil snarled. "Put the knife down—NOW."

Justin hesitated. "Let me . . . I can explain . . ."

"Shut up and do what I said." With a metallic click, Phil cocked the hammer on his Klock. "Slow—nice and easy like. Lower it to the floor in your hand with your palm up."

Jodi watched as Justin reluctantly yielded. Rather than drop the knife, he did as he was instructed. His movements were as slow as a snail's pace. His facial expression was devoid of hostility. He appeared resolved. She knew he had no real choice.

Phil said, "Now, slide the knife gently toward me. No monkey business." He still had Justin in his cross hairs. "And keep your hands where I can see them."

Justin complied. He bent over and with one hand slid the knife across the linoleum. It stopped within a few inches of Phil's shoes. Phil placed his foot on the handle of the knife. His gun remained on target.

Justin raised both arms, though the weight of his knee still applied pressure to the small of Stan's back.

Jodi breathed a sigh of relief. She felt compelled to report what she had heard. "I . . . I was in my room when I heard these terrible . . ."

". . . screams coming . . ." Heather started to join in.

Phil cut them off. "Shut up, Jodi. You too," he said with a sharp nod toward Heather. "Nobody moves. Nobody talks. Unless I say so. Got it?"

He turned to Bruce. "You . . . turn on the light in the galley."

Bruce reached for the switch. Nothing.

Stan coughed, still facedown. "Bulbs . . . they're in the trash . . . Hey, I'm losing blood over here . . ."

"I said, shut up, Stan. I've got eyes," Phil said sharply.

Jodi saw the puzzled look on Bruce's face.

Phil spoke. "Go ahead, Bruce. Check it out."

A moment later Bruce had a light bulb working in the galley. Phil switched off his flashlight and crouched to retrieve the knife.

"Justin—I want you facedown on the ground next to Stan, hands behind your back," Phil ordered.

"If you'll just give me a minute to explain . . ."

"You're the *last* one I intend to listen to. Facedown!"

Justin shook his head in disbelief before lying down as instructed. Phil placed the gun in his waistband.

Jodi was amazed at how quickly Phil moved to secure the room. With the knife, Phil cut several lengths of cord, each two feet long, from the window's miniblinds. He tied together Justin's arms, and then his legs. He repeated the process with Stan. As he dressed Stan's wound, Phil assured him that, while it produced heavy bleeding, it was just a minor scrape.

Meanwhile, Bruce, following Phil's instructions, swept up the broken bits of glass and raised the window coverings.

"Listen, people," Phil announced, "I want the girls to take a seat on the sofa. No talking. Bruce, tell Carlos it's safe to come out of his room; then you and he will sit on the folding chairs."

Phil stood in the middle of the room as he took command.

Justin and Stan, hands and feet still tied, sat adjacent to the kitchen table.

As Jodi made her way to the sofa she thought that Stan, oddly, appeared defeated. His broad shoulders slumped. His eyes were fixed on the floor in a blank stare. Something else bothered her about Stan. She expected him to be—or to at least look—grateful now that Phil had saved his life. What gives? Maybe he was drained from the whole ordeal. She knew she would be if the roles had been reversed. But her instincts nagged; something wasn't quite right with this picture.

Jodi took her seat and glanced at Justin, who, for the first time, seemed visibly alert, even upbeat. What a contrast, she thought, to his otherwise withdrawn, dark persona throughout the trip. What was it she detected behind his eyes? Relief?

A minute later, Bruce and Carlos took their places.

Phil crossed his arms and glared at Stan.

"Why don't you tell me what this is all about?"

4:21 A.M.
Abington, Pennsylvania

With the exception of *Pro Golf Digest*, Rosie Meyer had just finished reading virtually every magazine in the waiting room at Abington Memorial Hospital. She had even glanced at the hospital's annual report—anything to pass the time. She learned the facility, founded in 1914, had 508 beds. The Toll Pavilion at Abington Hospital, where Rosie awaited a medical update on Kat's condition, was one of the more recent buildings. The Coast Guard had taken them there last night.

During the forty-five-minute helicopter flight, the Guard explained that this state-of-the-art critical care unit was unmatched in the region. After they landed on the rooftop helipad, a team of emergency personnel took over and raced Kat down the dedicated elevator to the ground floor for a battery of tests.

For Rosie, who had been up all night, the whole experience was one big, painful blur. She sank down in her chair, crossed her legs, and leaned her head back against the red brick wall. Her eyelids were heavy with sleep, but a nap was out of the question. Not with Kat struggling to hold on to life in the trauma unit. Yet, emotionally drained, she had to close her eyes for a minute. *This trip has turned into such a nightmare*, she thought.

Although she tried to relax, her mind drifted to yesterday, to the moment when the surgeon broke the news.

"Mrs. Meyer, let me be candid. I need to remove Kat's left kidney—immediately," he had said. "Kat's pretty banged up. She's lost a lot of blood. And, assuming no complications, that only gets us halfway home. We're going to need to find a donor to replace her right kidney or she won't make it. Be assured we are doing everything possible to see her through this."

Did the doctor really say, "Kat might not make it"? she thought. *Is he serious? Kat could die?* The reality didn't hit Rosie until he added, "We need for you to sign the release documents as the responsible party."

As Rosie signed the paperwork, she recalled how, for the first time in years, she was tempted to pray—but didn't. She wasn't sure how—or what—to pray. She felt like a hypocrite, anyway, unsure if God would listen since she hadn't been to Mass in decades. Was that why she hesitated to call out to God? Or was there something more, something deeper? Then it dawned on her. The truth was she didn't trust that God would answer her petition and couldn't deal with the disappointment . . . just as he didn't answer her prayers to stop her alcoholic dad from beating her. The memory chilled her.

She opened her eyes. On the end table to her right sat her neglected, lukewarm cup of decaf coffee in a Styrofoam container.

She reached for it, took a sip, and swallowed hard. Three creamers and two packets of sweetener did little to improve its taste. "What did you expect from a vending machine?" the receptionist said when Rosie complained.

She stood up, carried the cup to the trash can, then rambled around the waiting room to examine the generic pictures mounted on the wall—for the third time. And yet, for the first time her attention was drawn to a sketch of a marina. She stood before it, folded her arms, and pictured Phil and the students out on the houseboat.

She wondered how they were getting along without her to help them process this tragedy. *Jodi is probably using Kat's misfortune to hold a revival meeting,* she thought. *That's the problem. Jodi's faith comes too easy for her. She's young. Her faith would probably cave in if God asked something hard of her.*

"Mrs. Meyer?"

Rosie turned around. She hadn't heard the doctor approach.

"Yes? I'm Mrs. Meyer."

"Dr. Tim Johnson." He extended his hand. "I'm the ER doctor on call tonight." They shook hands.

"How's Kat?" Rosie searched his eyes. "I'm so worried about her."

He held a clipboard but didn't need to consult it. "Her vital signs have stabilized and she's resting comfortably, though heavily sedated, which is normal considering what she's been through."

"I see. Is there anything I can do?"

"Actually, yes. I realize you tried earlier to get in contact with her parents. Any luck?"

Rosie bit the inside of her lip. "Is there a problem you're not telling me?"

"No. What I mean to say, Kat's blood type . . ."

". . . is AB-negative and is in critically short supply," Rosie finished his sentence. She wanted to say, "Tell me something I don't already know," but thought better of it.

"Correct. And, as you also know, we must locate a donor match to replace her right kidney. A member of her family is usually the best place to look for either additional blood or a living organ donor."

Rosie shook her head. "That's gonna be a problem in this case. Her father is in prison over in Jersey, and her mom is a bit of a free spirit."

Dr. Johnson appeared puzzled. "Could you be more specific?"

"Guess that's the nice way of saying her mother is somewhat of a recreational drug abuser, so she's probably not a viable option. Besides, Kat told me that her mom took the bus down to Atlantic City to hang out at the casinos. She's out of touch for the rest of this week, maybe longer."

He gripped his clipboard with both hands. Rosie thought he appeared to be weighing what he was about to say.

"Mrs. Meyer, I don't know how else to put this . . ."

She sensed his discomfort. "How about the truth?"

"Kat doesn't have that much time. And we're running out of options."

4:25 A.M.

"It was like this," Stan started to explain without looking up. "I was hungry, you know. Um, we didn't have much of a dinner last night, what with Kat's accident and all. A guy's gotta eat, so I figured I'd sneak into the kitchen—I mean the galley—and grab a little snack or something, but then this psycho jumped me—"

"I did *not*—"

"Shut up, Justin." Phil shot him an icy look.

"Hey, maybe he thinks he's the food police, I don't know." Stan made a half-turn with his head in the direction of Justin. He didn't make eye contact.

"If you'd just let me explain . . ."

Phil jabbed a finger in the direction of Justin's face. "Don't you realize this isn't a game? I call the shots and I'm telling you, Justin, not another word."

Stan cleared his throat. "I was sitting here at the table when he plowed into my side, knocked me out of the chair—"

"He's lying!"

Phil took a step toward Stan and Justin then slammed his clenched fist on the surface of the galley table between them. "I cannot think of one good reason why your mouth should be moving, Justin. Am I clear? Or do I need to tape your trap shut?"

Justin's eyes widened.

Stan continued. "I've been tackled before, but never by a crazy guy with a knife, otherwise I could have taken him out with my own hands," he raised his bound wrists for emphasis. "As it was, I could have been killed by this freak, ya know what I'm saying? Then who knows . . . maybe, well, maybe he planned to slaughter the rest of you in your sleep."

Justin shook his head violently in disagreement and blurted out, "I'm trying to tell you, Stan is suicidal . . . *that's* what the knife was for."

At that, Phil grabbed the first aid kit and yanked out a thick roll of gauze. Jodi was sure Phil was about to gag Justin.

But Justin shouted, "If you don't believe me, read his note. It's over there in the corner."

Jodi saw Stan's face redden.

Stan said, "See what I mean, the guy's mental. Anybody can tell that, right, guys?" He looked at Bruce and Carlos for support.

Phil hesitated for a split second to look in the direction where Justin was nodding. Jodi followed his eyes as he spotted a single sheet of paper on the floor. She figured it had drifted there during the scuffle.

"Jodi, would you get that for me, please?" Phil asked.

"Sure thing." She retrieved the note, and then handed it to Phil. Stan's face turned pale.

Justin's tone softened. "Stan, come on. Why don't you tell them what this was *really* about?"

Stan slumped forward, his head resting on his hands, and started to sob. Jodi looked around the room as they watched him fight to control this outburst of emotion and to hide his grief. But his large frame shook as the tears continued to flow.

Jodi figured Stan must be holding on to some dark secret, buried deep inside. She was the first to speak, slowly at first. "Stan . . . what's the matter?"

He didn't look up.

"Whatever it is . . . just let it out," Jodi said with genuine compassion.

Stan's tears rolled freely down his face.

"Justin's right. That's my knife. I . . . I was gonna kill myself . . . had it all planned out . . . would have cut my wrists too 'cept Justin stopped me."

Jodi felt the air in her lungs tighten. "But why?"

He wiped away the tears with his bound hands and then looked up toward the ceiling. He appeared embarrassed by what he was about to confess.

"A couple of years ago, my younger brother, Bobby, and three of his friends were horsing around in our backyard. They'd been messing around with a few moves they picked up from one of those stupid pro-wrestling shows . . . I'm not sure which. Doesn't matter. Anyway, at some point the fun got really violent . . . they started doing the clothesline and the smack down . . . things kinda got out of hand."

His bottom lip started to tremble. He took a deep breath to regain his composure.

"When I got home from football practice, I went to the kitchen to make a protein shake. Through the open kitchen window, I could hear my brother and his friends talkin' trash—crazy stuff, like they do in that fake wrestling baloney. I started to go outside to see what all the yelling was about, but . . . I don't know why, I . . . I decided to first look through the window."

He closed his eyes at the memory.

"When I looked, Bobby was on the ground. The three boys had surrounded him. They were pounding and kicking Bobby's head. He even looked right at me, his . . . his eyes were swollen and, well, that's when I . . . I froze . . ."

Stan looked at the group. More tears. He wiped his nose with his forearm. "Don't ask me why. I just froze."

He sat silently for a moment.

"You know, I could have broken the whole thing up easy. I was way bigger than those punks. Still, I hesitated long enough that my brother suffered a serious head injury. I never told my parents—or anyone—how I failed my only brother that afternoon."

Jodi, like Heather and Vanessa, was in tears. As Stan spoke, she wanted to say something, anything, to comfort him. "Oh, Stan . . . We all make mistakes. That's no reason to give up on life."

Stan started to rock back and forth.

"Bobby died three days later in the hospital."

Outside, a distant thunderclap hammered the sky. The downpour intensified.

"Don't you see? It was all my fault! How could I live with what I had done?" Stan searched their faces. "And each time one of the guys on the team called me 'Stan da man,' this pain shot through me. I knew I was nothing more than a big coward. So I pushed myself on the field . . . used girls for the sex . . . did a little alcohol . . . I did anything I could to kill this awful feeling. The way I see it, I didn't deserve to live . . . I still don't, either."

Stan shifted in his seat to face Justin. They exchanged glances for a moment.

"How did you know, Justin? I mean, how'd you know I was

gonna . . ." His voice trailed off. "You couldn't have seen what was in my note."

Justin looked at Phil as if requesting permission to speak. Phil nodded. "You're right. I didn't see what you wrote down. That was just a lucky guess on my part."

Stan appeared puzzled.

Justin continued. "About six, maybe seven weeks ago, I got a note from Faith Morton. I'm told you two were an item until she broke up with you, right? Anyway, something you said, or maybe the way you acted, convinced her that you were suicidal. Remember how she was going on this trip but decided against it once you guys broke up? That's when you said you'd be going on the houseboat but wouldn't be coming back . . . and she'd be sorry she dumped you. Something like that."

"Yeah, I might have said that," Stan said.

"She read between the lines but didn't want to overreact and cause a scene. It wasn't like she had any real proof, just a feeling. She begged me to come on this trip—even offered to pay my way. I promised her I'd watch out for you and I'd do my best to keep you from . . . well, you know, just in case you planned to take your life."

Justin paused then added, "I understand your feelings, Stan. When I was old enough to understand what happened to my parents, how they were murdered in Pakistan as missionaries, I was mad at God, you know? I was the only kid who didn't have either of his real parents around. Things didn't make sense and I wanted to end my life too. My first foster parents helped me get over some of that."

Stan listened intently.

"But there's something else," Justin said. "I wasn't sure my new foster parents would let me come, so I forged my parental permission slip. They don't know where I am."

Phil shook his head in disgust as he used the knife to cut their bonds. "Brilliant."

"Why did you do that?" Bruce asked his roommate.

"I don't know. Just a precaution. I couldn't risk them saying no, not after I promised Faith I'd watch Stan."

Jodi said, "Don't you think they're worried sick, Justin?"

"You're right. After all they've done for me, I should have been honest with them," Justin said then fell silent.

In the quiet of the moment, another thunderbolt, this time much closer, rumbled across the sky.

Jodi almost bounded out of her seat.

"Phil—"

He looked up from cutting Justin free.

"I almost forgot about Kat! Last night I prayed about—oops, sorry—I arrived at a decision. I want to offer Kat one of my kidneys, that is, if she still needs it."

Heather put her arm around Jodi. With a supportive hug, she said, "Really? Wow—I'm so proud of you."

Vanessa, her hands folded in her lap, appeared reserved. "Are you sure you want to do this, Jodi? I mean, I'm happy for Kat and all, but it's such a big deal. I don't understand how anyone could make that sacrifice."

Jodi flashed her a warm smile. "Like I said, I really believe God wants me to do this for Kat. That's really all there is to it. So, Phil," she said, looking back in Phil's direction, "I need to use the cell phone to call my parents for permission. If they agree, I'll call the hospital too. May I?"

Phil thought for a moment. "The cell phone isn't an option."

"Why not?" Jodi said, hooking her hair behind her ears.

"Rosie took it with her. We'll just use the radio to reach the Coast Guard. They can make the connections for you."

Stan started to sob a second time.

Within an instant, all eyes were fixed on him.

"Now what?" Carlos asked.

"The radio is dead . . . I cut the antenna so you wouldn't be able to call for help once I . . ." His voice faltered. "I didn't want anyone rescuing me, you know? And, um, I sliced the gas line on the powerboat for . . . for the same reason. Gosh, what have I done? What if I cause the death of Kat? I'm such a fool . . ."

"Oh, that's just perfect, you stupid idiot," Carlos started to say.

"Hey, we'll have none of that," Phil said.

"Well—the way I see it, we've got no phone, no radio, no powerboat, and in case you haven't noticed, there's a storm brewing," Carlos said, crossing his arms. "Plus, Kat may be dying at this very minute. So what do you suggest now?"

Jodi half expected Phil to gag Carlos, but he appeared to overlook the insulting tone. Phil checked his watch; Jodi checked her watch too. It was just after 5 A.M., and daylight, or what little of it could be seen through the cloud covering, would soon be dawning.

Phil leaned against the galley counter and enumerated the options out loud for the group. None were particularly hopeful.

First, he explained he could try and repair the antenna, but that would be tricky in the middle of the storm without the right tools and without additional cable. Even if he managed to restore the connection, the radio might need to be recalibrated.

Second, they could head for the nearest shore point, but that could still take a couple of hours from their present position.

Third, Justin could take Jodi to shore in the small powerboat, but not with the gas line cut and no means to repair it.

After a long moment, Jodi spoke up.

"I know you guys may think I'm way out of line here. But why don't we pray about it?" She offered a smile. "I happen to believe God still works miracles. And, let's just say, in the spirit of tolerance, why don't we give my personal conviction a try?"

She looked first at Phil then at the others.

"Hey, I'm not gonna stop ya," Phil said returning her smile with one of his own. The others nodded in agreement.

Jodi bowed her head and began to pray aloud.

6:55 A.M.

"Okay, people, here's our situation." Phil stood at the door to the hallway. He scanned the faces of the students who sat around the kitchen table. Some drank coffee, others tea or juice. They had just finished a light breakfast thrown together by Jodi and Heather.

"Coffee?" Jodi poured a fresh cup and held it out to Phil.

He wiped his hands on his jeans and took the cup. "Thank you." He took a sip. "You must be wondering why we haven't started to sail for shore yet."

Several heads nodded.

"I've just spent more than an hour attempting to retract the anchor. But the windlass is acting up again so I can't dislodge the anchor."

"I thought you fixed that yesterday," Carlos said, his brow furrowed.

"That's what I thought," Phil said. "Can't be sure, but my guess is the roughness of the bay waters jarred the chain and the windlass assembly enough to jam the mechanism."

Jodi considered this. Why would God put it on her heart to help Kat then make it impossible to get to Kat? *Maybe he was just testing my heart to see if I was willing,* Jodi thought. Maybe she wouldn't have to make this sacrifice after all. Did that mean God had some other way of helping Kat? She twirled several strands of hair as she thought. She looked at Phil. "What about the power-boat? Can you fix whatever's wrong with it?"

"I checked that too. Stan did a first-class job butchering the supply hose. The powerboat is definitely out of commission."

Stan cursed at himself. "Guess I've really ruined everything now."

For a moment, nobody spoke.

Bruce scratched his head. "So we're stuck and there's no way for Jodi to get to shore?"

"There *is* one other option," Phil said. He set his cup on the table.

Jodi noticed the others were just as riveted on Phil as she was.

"It's too far to swim, so what do you have in mind?" Carlos asked.

"The WaveRunners, unless you crippled them too," Phil said with a look in the direction of Stan.

For the first time all morning, Stan actually smiled. "Believe it or not, I forgot about them."

"Good . . . ," Phil started to say.

"Whoa . . . wait a minute," Jodi said, placing both hands on the table. "You want me to do what? Ride one of those to shore? You can't be serious . . . I . . ." Jodi crossed her arms and sat back in her chair. "Well, I've never been on one, and those waves don't look friendly to me." She stared at Phil.

Phil raised his hands as if in self-defense. "I certainly wouldn't want you to feel like you had to take one. I'm just presenting the option." He lowered his hands and picked up his coffee. "For what it's worth, two people can ride one. If someone else volunteered to drive, you could ride on back."

He's not serious, Jodi thought as she watched him sip his beverage. "I . . . I don't know, Phil. That's way too crazy."

Heather didn't give Phil a chance to respond. "Hey, I'd be willing to take her."

Jodi wasn't sure whether to thank or hit her friend. "Yeah, but what about the storm?" Jodi asked. Her forefinger began a nervous tap on the tabletop.

"Let's just say if you act fast, I believe you can outrun the worst of the weather. Right now it's just raining and the waves are less than two feet. A WaveRunner can handle that—no problem," Phil said. "I've owned one for years and you'll do fine."

"Hold on a second," Carlos said. "We've all heard the thunder and lightning in the distance, right? You mean to tell me that's no biggie?" He shook his head as if in disbelief.

"You want the truth? We're gonna be in greater danger on this boat than they will be out there." Phil pointed out the window at the choppy water. "The way we're positioned in the bay, when the waves reach four or five feet—and from what I've been told they will with this storm, maybe more—we could be flipped like a pancake."

Jodi crossed her legs and folded her arms as if a cold draft blew through the room.

"For real? How so?" Carlos asked then chewed his bottom lip.

"At the moment, our boat is facing beam to the wind."

Bruce cocked an eyebrow. "Exsqueeze me?"

"Beam to the wind . . . that's when the widest part of the ship is pointed toward the direction of the waves," Phil said. "We really need to be bow to the wind so that the waves crash against the front of the ship rather than the side."

"So why can't you just turn the boat?" Carlos asked.

"Unless we can retract the anchor, we can't change position."

"Let me get this straight," Carlos said. "We're about to get smacked by a monsoon and you're gonna send Jodi out there in a WaveRunner? Am I missing something? And like, what about us? Shouldn't we be worrying about saving ourselves instead of worrying about Kat, who's safe inside a hospital?"

"For your information, Carlos," Phil said, his tone was direct, "the storm is moving from east to west. That means the thunder is coming from the east. Rather than heading into the storm, Jodi will travel away from it in a westward direction. Believe me, I wouldn't make the suggestion if there was a great risk. As for saving ourselves"—Phil suppressed a cough—"I've been trained to take care of the wounded first, then the healthy. That's what we're doing."

Jodi sat without talking for a long minute. The falling rain and a steady tapping on the aluminum hull of the houseboat by the agitated water were the only sounds in the room, except for an occasional thunderclap in the distance. In the near silence she whispered a prayer for strength.

"How long would it take?" Jodi said finally.

"You're not serious, are you?" Carlos said.

She ignored him. "How long, Phil?"

Phil cocked his head. "That's a 1990 LX model. Top speed is probably forty miles an hour. With two people and choppy water . . . I'd say you'll probably do about half of that speed. You're looking at just over half an hour. At most forty minutes."

Heather sat forward. "Jodi, we can do it . . . I know we can."

Jodi looked at her then studied the faces of each person in the room as if gathering votes.

Phil checked his watch and said, "Jodi, you need to make a decision. Time is not on our side this morning."

"I know . . . I know." Jodi exhaled a heavy sigh. "All right. Okay. There doesn't seem to be any other way, so"—she ran her hands through her hair—"let's do it."

"But, Jodi," Phil said, "I want one of the guys to take you." His eyes glanced between Jodi and Heather.

"Wait a minute. That's not fair," Heather said with a huff.

"It's nothing personal, Heather," Phil said. "I want the strongest person up front in case the water gets rough. So, guys, who's it gonna be?"

"Count me out," Carlos said waving his right hand in the air. "Hey, there's no law against being a dimwit. But I don't plan to be one. I'm not going out in that mess."

"I'll do it," Stan offered.

Phil shook his head no. "Stan, you're wounded, remember?"

Stan reached and felt his bandaged side. "It's just a scratch—remember?"

"How about it, Justin . . . Bruce?" Phil asked.

After a moment, Justin raised his chin. "I'm game. I've used one before. I'd like to help . . . sure."

Heather said to Jodi, "I wish I were going with ya." She patted Jodi on the back.

"I know."

"Don't worry, you'll do great. Those WaveRunners are un-sinkable," Heather said.

"Hey, isn't that what they said about the *Titanic?*" Bruce asked with a smirk.

Heather threw a crumpled napkin at him. "Dorkus!"

Justin and Jodi had placed their tennis shoes in the watertight stor-age compartment. Each wore a swimsuit and an orange life pre-server. Both were soaked by the steady rain as they sat on the WaveRunner, which bobbed in place by the rear of the house-boat.

Jodi focused intently on Phil, who sat on the rear deck, as he clipped a twenty-inch nylon cord from the WaveRunner handle-bar to Justin's vest. "What's that for?" she asked.

"This is connected to the engine kill switch. If Justin falls off, this stops the engine," Phil said. "That way the craft won't race off without you. And, as you already know, this is salt water. If you do fall in—don't swallow . . . and stay together."

"I'm so glad I asked," Jodi said under her breath; her heart started to pound as if she had just finished the Boston marathon.

"Now, do you see those two flashing red lights off in the distance?" Phil pointed to a tower in the west. "There's one at thirty feet above sea level, the other is thirty feet or so directly above the lower light."

Justin and Jodi both squinted then nodded.

"Those lights are on a radio tower near the marina. That's your mark. Don't take your eyes off of it. At sea level, it's easy to lose your sense of direction—especially without a compass. We don't want you heading out to sea, do we?"

Jodi swallowed hard. Her stomach started to churn as if pro-cessing a batch of greasy fries.

"And Justin, no hot-dogging around. I'm counting on you to get Jodi to shore." Phil looked him directly in the eyes. "If the waves get too choppy, don't be a hero. Get your butt back here. Am I clear?"

"Got it." Justin flashed a thumbs-up.

Jodi sat on the back of the WaveRunner as stiff as an over-starched shirt. Although still unnerved by the whole experience, she liked the way Phil's voice was packed with authority.

Phil turned to Jodi. His voice softened a notch. "Getting to Kat is really important to both you and her, right?"

"Of course . . . why do you ask?" She looked down to double-check the fasteners on her life vest.

"Don't ever lose sight of that fact. No matter what. Fight to make it happen. Got it?"

She looked up and met his eyes. "Sure thing."

Jodi took a deep breath. She started to fiddle with her soaked hair as a new series of thoughts bothered her. What was Phil trying to say? Would she get to shore, or would she fall off and drown? Was that it? What if the storm got any worse? The dark cloud covering made it hard to see where they were headed. What if they got lost? What about lightning? Could they get electrocuted? And if they made it to shore, would they get to Kat in time?

"Something wrong?" Phil asked.

"Um, I guess I would've preferred something from you like, 'Enjoy the ride.'"

Phil raised an eyebrow. "Okay, think of this as a roller-coaster ride at Hershey Park. Have fun."

Jodi rolled her eyes. "Oh, that's great . . . I *hate* roller coasters."

7:20 A.M.
Huntingdon Valley, Pennsylvania

John Crans had not gotten much sleep after receiving a middle-of-the-night call from Rosie Meyer confirming Justin was indeed on the houseboat and informing him that Kat's condition was stable but critical. To make matters worse, the houseboat still remained out of radio contact.

He had arrived at his office before dawn, polished off two cups of coffee, paced the floor, shuffled a few papers, downed another cup of the black liquid, checked his e-mail, and then sat at his desk, where he stroked his unshaven face as he stared at the phone. After a few minutes, he glanced at his watch, snatched up the phone handset, and punched in a series of numbers.

"Bay Rentals, Joey here."

"It's John Crans. You're in early," he said, trying to be polite. "Thought I'd have to leave a message."

"Nah, we're here at seven. So how can I help you this fine, rainy day?"

"You never called me back last night."

"Oh, yeah. Well, um, we couldn't contact the boat. Remember, the radio is dead."

"What about the Coast Guard? Couldn't you have found out from them what happened?" John gripped the handset tightly, his words crackled the air.

"I . . . gee . . . you seem upset," Joey said. "What's the deal?"

"We may have a serious situation on our hands. Got a call last night from Rosie Meyer. She confirmed that Justin Moore is on board the houseboat."

"Great. So now you know where the lost kid is."

John rubbed his face with his free hand. "Listen, Joey. I need you to contact the Coast Guard and request that they find that boat—immediately."

"Sure. Sure. But I gotta tell ya, the Guard isn't a babysitting service. You got to give 'em a good reason to search the bay with this storm coming."

John started to drum his fingers on the desktop. "Justin is probably armed—and may be dangerous. Someone's life might be at stake."

"Why didn't you say so?"

"I just did." John spat the words through clenched teeth, trying to control his frustration. "Now, either you call this minute or give me the number and contact person and I'll call. What's it going to be?"

"I gotcha covered. And don't worry, the Guard has an active arsenal on board. They'll know what to do."

John was about to hang up. "Oh, and Joey . . . this time, call me back with the details, okay?"

"Sure, sure."

7:37 A.M.

"Do you have to go so fast?" Jodi had to raise her voice to be heard over the high-strung whine of the 650 cc engine. The constant drone of the rain and the distant thunder added to the chaotic mixture of noise.

"Trust me, this isn't fast." He turned his head slightly toward his left shoulder as he spoke, keeping one eye on the tower. Both hands were fixed on the handlebars. A blast of water hit the side of his face as a wave slapped the front of the WaveRunner. "Any slower and I'm afraid we'll stall out," he shouted.

Her arms, like a vise grip, were clamped around Justin's waist. She strained to keep an eye on the tower lights, but the sky, gray and overcast like a thick blanket, made visibility difficult.

"Are we almost there?" Jodi said.

"No way. It's only been maybe ten minutes."

"Seems like forever."

No sooner had she spoken than a series of waves rocked them from the side. Justin turned a sharp left, then jogged to the right to stabilize. He twisted the throttle, sending a burst of gas to the engine as they hit another wave head-on. They bounced hard on the seat just as a rolling wave slammed them with enough force to toss them and the four-hundred-pound machine two feet into the air. The fiberglass body pounded the bay waters with a smack.

Jodi struggled to catch her breath. After a long moment, Jodi said, "How's your butt?"

This time Justin turned his head almost completely around, taking his eyes off of the tower for a split second in the process. "What kind of question is that?"

I don't know about you—mine's sore as a monkey," she said.

An instant later, Justin yelled, "Lean left . . . now right . . ." The engine whined as he worked to maneuver the craft.

"You're good, Justin."

"Thanks. I've been out before . . . my buddy owns a SeaDoo. Same idea."

A deep thunderclap, this time much closer, caused Jodi to let out a shriek. "Whoa—that was too close! You sure we're headed in the right direction?"

He nodded straight ahead. "Yeah. See? There's the light."

She strained to catch a glimpse. "I only see one flashing light."

"I'm sure that's it. Clouds gotta be hiding the other one."

"Justin!" Jodi's eyes widened as the water in front of them reared back like a snake about to strike. Seconds later, a four-foot wall of water heaved and then crashed directly in their path, causing the little craft to bounce wildly.

Her grip on Justin's waist tightened. Her legs pinched the body of the WaveRunner as if she were riding a wild bronco. She shouted, "We'll never make it."

"Just hang on!" With that, Justin zigged to the right, zagged to the left, and gunned the engine. Jodi could see he was working to avoid a head-on, frontal assault by a Goliath-like wave gathering strength before her eyes. But it was too little, too late. The powerful blast of water made Jodi feel as if they were being pushed backward.

On any other occasion, the frothy brew of bay water splashing against their faces might have been a welcome relief from a hot sun. Today, however, with no visible sunlight, it was a salty irritant that made Jodi almost vomit. She turned her head to the side, coughed out a mouthful of water, and then shot a look forward.

"Where's the light?" Jodi yelled.

"Wait a second . . . over there . . . that's it." With a lurch, he goosed the engine once again, this time aiming more directly for the blinking red light in the distance.

Jodi strained to see. Something about the light bothered her. It appeared to be too low. With a sharp yet futile side-to-side motion, Jodi shook her head, hoping to shake the veil of water and hair that partially obscured her view. *That was pointless*, she thought. She didn't dare let go of Justin—even with one hand—long enough to pull the clumps of hair plastered across her face.

A minute later, she decided to wipe her face against the back of Justin's life vest. She squinted. Like a slow Internet download, it finally dawned on her what she was staring at.

"Justin . . . that's *not* the light!"

"Sure it is."

"No," she shouted back. "It's too low . . . that's a buoy! I'm telling ya we're headed in the wrong direction!"

Justin swore.

She felt the WaveRunner slow down to something just above an idle. Neither spoke for a long minute as the waves kicked them around like a tin can on a sidewalk. A bolt of lightning struck the surface of the water in the distance. At the sound, her chest heaved as it tried to contain the pounding of her heart.

"Which way back?" she yelled.

"Can't tell. Hold on." Justin put the two-seater into a circular pattern. "See the boat?"

"Can't you?"

Justin shook his head no.

She struggled to fight off the sudden ripple of panic. Like a thief it stole her breath. She gasped for air. Where was the houseboat? What if the engine stalled? What if they ran out of gas? What if they couldn't find their way? How deep was the water? How long could she tread water?

She pinched her eyes shut for a long second, hoping this was just a bad dream. Just then a picture of Kat, still strapped to the stretcher, surfaced in her mind. The desperate look in Kat's eyes; her limp, banged-up, and bruised body; the way she pleaded, "Pray for me" as the Coast Guard carted her off . . . the memories, with a jolt, released some inner reservoir of strength. They just *had* to get to Kat, she thought.

She opened her eyes and cried out, "Jesus . . . *Jesus!* . . . get us back . . ."

Phil was at the helm in the upper wheelhouse, studying their coordinates. Bruce was at his side using the binoculars to follow the movements of Justin and Jodi. Both were wearing life vests. So were the other students, who, taking orders from Phil, sat on the floor in the main cabin below.

Phil said, "What do you see?"

Bruce hesitated. "It's hard to tell. They were doing fine, but . . . hold on, I lost them . . . wait, there they are. I'd say it looks as if they're going in a circle. Gosh, and that water is real choppy."

"Here, let me have a look," Phil said, taking the binoculars from Bruce. "You're right. They must be disoriented. Get the emergency kit. Quickly. It's in the cabinet next to the captain's chair." Phil kept the optical device trained on the WaveRunner as he dealt out the order.

"Okay, now what?" Bruce said. He retrieved a metal box, about the size of a large briefcase with bold red lettering denoting the contents, and then snapped open two hasp fasteners on the front edge.

"Look for a flare gun with at least two rounds. Do you see it?"

Bruce moved aside several items. Encased in a foam-padded corner, he found the gun and flares. "Got 'em."

"Here. Let's trade. Don't lose sight of them."

Bruce pressed the goggles to his face.

Phil examined the flare and was pleased to notice it was a parachute flare. "Great. This will hang in the sky hopefully long enough to do the trick. I want you to tell me the moment they start to turn in our direction—understood?"

"Yes sir."

Phil took the flare gun, loaded one round in the chamber, stepped outside onto the fly bridge, pointed skyward, and waited.

Twenty seconds later, Bruce said, "Now!"

Phil pulled the trigger. With a powerful boom, a brilliant burst of yellow-and-orange flame exploded fifty feet overhead. The wavering light lingered in the sky as a trail of spent particles drifted downward.

"You see that?" Jodi said.

"See what? Where?"

"Fireworks. To the left."

Justin craned his neck. "It looks more like a flare . . . That's gotta be the houseboat!"

For the first time in what seemed an eternity, Jodi experienced a surge of hope. "Thank you, God," she said under her breath.

"Hold on tight," Justin shouted.

With a lurch, she felt him rev the engine for all it was worth. They shot forward like a bullet fired from a sawed-off shotgun. Together, they leaned forward into the wind as the blue-and-silver WaveRunner cut a hasty path to the boat.

Eight minutes later, Justin backed off the throttle enough to be heard over the engine's drone. He leaned back and said, "Almost there. Maybe fifty yards or so. You okay?"

"Just peachy."

What else could she say? Truth was—her fingers had swollen up like prune skins, her arms ached from holding on so tightly, she had a nasty cramp in her right middle toe, her heart felt bruised from beating so hard, her bum started to go numb from the pounding against the seat each time an angry wave swatted them . . . not to mention she never felt so waterlogged in all her life.

But she had hope. Right now, that was enough.

She sensed Justin felt hopeful too, now that the houseboat was clearly in view. It was maybe the length of half a football field away, she guessed. In a playful tone Justin leaned back and said, "You wanna drive the rest of the way?"

Jodi smiled and said, "Not on your life, buddy." On impulse, she sat upright, released her grip on Justin's waist, and with a friendly tease, started to swat him on the back.

But before she could regain her grip on his waist, the WaveRunner bolted ahead. Justin, trying to avoid being broadsided by a wave, had punched the engine. She was completely unprepared for the forward thrust; her body jerked backward, bringing her legs about even with the seat. A lateral wave clobbered her, knocking her off the watercraft.

As she fell, a fresh burst of lightning ripped across the dark morning sky, followed by a sudden downpour of heavy rain. She plunged into the salty blackness. The last thing she saw was Justin; he had turned sharply to grab her foot only to lose his own balance, then he, too, fell from the WaveRunner.

Jodi thrashed helplessly underwater. The overhead thunder was nothing but a dull, muted sound now. The cramp in her toe fought her efforts to find the surface of the water. Which way was up? How far was down? Her lungs begged for just another breath as her eyes throbbed in unison with her overtaxed heart. Fighting the swirling undertow sapped what little strength she had left.

"*I tried, Kat . . .*" was the last thing Jodi thought before she blacked out.

"Phil . . . *Phil!*"

"Something wrong, Bruce?" Phil said evenly. He looked up from his charts of the Chesapeake Bay at Bruce, who was stationed by the window.

"Oh my *gosh* . . . they've flipped . . . there's Justin, but I can't see Jodi . . . oh, wait, there she is."

With a quick, sure movement, Phil stood and moved to Bruce's side. "I'll take those," Phil said, reaching for the binoculars. He pressed his face to the field glasses. An instant later he spotted Justin and Jodi. He noted their life vests kept them afloat, yet they were being tossed around by the waves like two rubber ducks.

"Go below. Get Carlos and Stan and the megaphone. Meet me on the rear deck in sixty seconds," Phil said.

"Are they gonna make it?"

"If you do exactly what I say . . . yes. Now hustle!"

Bruce turned and dashed down the aluminum ladder to the main deck.

Phil, in turn, hung the binoculars around his neck and walked to the opposite side of the wheelhouse, where he opened a compartment and removed a long, yellow nylon rope. He slung the rope over his left shoulder, snatched a life preserver off of the wall, and climbed down the ladder to the rear deck.

Once positioned on the deck, Phil tested the handrail along the side of the cabin and determined it was sturdy. He tied one end of the rope to the handrail, and then looped the opposite end around his waist, tying it securely in place. His movements, like a well-oiled machine, were smooth, quick, and efficient. Each action was polished from years of intense training.

He glanced over his shoulder and saw Bruce, Carlos, and Stan step through the rear door.

"Here, let me have the megaphone," Phil said to Bruce.

Bruce handed it to him.

Phil adjusted the volume. "Justin, can you hear me? If so, I want you to wave." Phil placed the binoculars to his eyes. A moment later, he saw Justin's signal. "Good. I'm coming for you. Meanwhile, if you can, get to Jodi. Hold on to each other and stay together. You'll be all right." Phil lowered the megaphone and, once he saw Justin swimming toward Jodi, he lowered the field glasses.

With a boom, a bolt of lightning darted across the sky. A moment later, a gust of wind, together with a five-foot wave, rocked the side of the houseboat with enough force to lift one edge of the boat partially out of the water. The boys collided into one another like the Three Stooges on a bad hair day and fell to the deck.

Carlos gripped the sliding board and staggered back up. "Are you crazy? You're not seriously going out there, are you?" His face paled.

Phil shot him a look. "Affirmative."

"You'll get hurt. Can't ya just toss them the life preserver or something?" Carlos said with both eyebrows raised. "I mean, like . . . what will happen to us?"

Phil ignored him. "Listen, guys. This is not a game. Justin and Jodi need us. You're going to do exactly what I tell you to do. And we've got one chance to get this right. Here's the plan. First, I want Stan . . ."

"Yes sir?"

"Take the binoculars and keep focused on Justin and Jodi. Don't let them out of your sight—even for a second. Clear?"

"Crystal." Stan took the binoculars and wrapped one arm around a pole for support as he focused on the situation. "Got 'em. Justin is almost to Jodi."

"Good. Hold on to the megaphone for me too." Phil handed it to Stan.

"Carlos and Bruce, your job is to retract the rope once I've reached Justin and Jodi. Then, once we're alongside of the boat, you need to lift them aboard," Phil said. "Maintain your balance by bracing yourself against the railing, like so." He demonstrated the proper position. "Trust me, if you're not careful, the force of the waves could drag you down."

Bruce nodded. "No problem."

"Actually," Phil said, "you have no concept of how powerful water can be. This operation will be touch and go. Remember, they're below your level, the waves will be working against you, and they'll feel like dead weight. So when the boat dips, use the momentum to yank them up onto the deck—like landing a fish. But wait until I give the signal. Got it?"

Bruce nodded.

Carlos just stared like a deer caught in a car's headlights.

After a short moment, Phil said, "Carlos, you can do this, son. We're a team, and none of us is going down. Not on my watch."

Carlos, his face still ashen, finally nodded.

"Okay. Take your positions. Stay focused. I'm going in." With that, Phil, still holding the life preserver, kicked off his shoes and jumped overboard.

Phil had been in rougher waters than this during his days as a Navy Seal. Yet he took no chances. He swam freestyle, his head always remaining above water to maintain constant awareness of Justin and Jodi's position. He knew panic, not the waves, was his worst enemy. If either of the students freaked out, they'd try to climb on top of him, which would jeopardize even his own safety. He wouldn't allow that to happen.

Several minutes of hard swimming placed him within five feet of Justin and Jodi. He stopped to tread water as he spoke. "Justin, stay calm. You're gonna be just fine. Do you trust me?"

Justin managed to nod. He was holding on to Jodi's life vest, though her head flopped around like a rag doll's.

"She looks . . . really pale . . ." Justin coughed out a mouthful of salt water along with his words.

Phil studied Jodi's condition for several seconds then said to Justin, "Listen to me, and we'll get through this. I'm going to throw you this life preserver. Place it over your head. Can you do that?" Phil didn't detect any panic in Justin's reaction.

"I'll sure try," Justin said, his face drained but focused.

Phil tossed him the device and watched Justin, with some effort, squeeze into it. Justin had to release Jodi for a few seconds as he put on the life preserver.

"Great. Now Jodi really needs our help. I want you to get a grip on her vest with your right hand and I want you to give me your left hand. We're gonna stay together and kick. Got it?"

Before Justin could respond, a wave slammed him from behind. The burst of water separated him from Jodi by several feet. His eyes widened as he gasped to catch his breath.

Phil shook his head. "Don't worry, I got her." Phil swam to Jodi, grabbed her vest from the side, and started to turn toward Justin when the force of an unseen object slammed Phil in the back of his neck; it stung but didn't cripple him. Phil glanced over his shoulder and saw Justin holding the life preserver like a weapon over his head. Justin's face appeared crazed, like a cornered cat ready to pounce.

Instinctively, Phil released Jodi, faced Justin, wrestled the preserver from him, and then grabbed Justin in a headlock. With a forceful dunk, Phil held Justin's head underwater for several long seconds. Although Phil felt Justin kicking and flailing beneath the surface of the water, his training confirmed there was no other way to overcome Justin's panic than to pretend to drown him.

Phil lifted Justin up for air.

Justin gasped, shook his head, and spat. "You crazy, man?"

"You listen to me . . . and listen good. I'm in charge here. Got it?" Phil dunked Justin again, this time longer.

Phil glanced over at Jodi. He had to make sure she didn't drift too far from reach. Finally, he brought Justin's head above the water.

Justin gagged, wheezed, and panted like a sick dog.

"Justin, look at me. Do what I say and everyone gets out alive. I'm going to tie this rope around you. Don't worry. Your life vest will keep you afloat. You won't have the use of your arms, so I want you to kick with your legs. Just wait until I give you the signal. If you don't comply, I promise you'll be blowing bubbles underwater again."

"I still say you're nuts, man," Justin said, his hair matted against his face making him look like a drenched rat.

Phil hooked the rope around Justin several times to constrain his arms from doing further damage. As it was, they'd already lost precious minutes. Phil then turned and swam to Jodi, who was beginning to appear bluish. He checked her pulse. She was breathing but unconscious. He put his arm around her waist and swam a few feet past Justin, where Phil gripped the rope with his free hand.

"Okay, Justin. Kick . . . *kick!*"

As the trio started to move toward the houseboat, Phil yelled, "Now—Bruce . . . Now—Carlos . . . pull, pull, *pull!*"

Phil eyed the houseboat with concern. The water was far more agitated than he'd anticipated. Worse, the boat careened erratically as the waves battered its broad side. If the boat pitched suddenly in the wrong direction while lifting Justin and Jodi onto the deck . . . He didn't want to consider that possibility.

"Okay—Bruce, Carlos—brace yourselves against the rail like I showed you," Phil commanded from the water. "This isn't a drill. This is for real. Take your spots—*now*."

Bruce got into position straddling the vertical stanchion and the horizontal lifeline. "I'm set."

Carlos didn't move.

"What's wrong?" Phil asked.

"I . . . I can't do this . . . ," Carlos said, his face white.

Phil didn't have time to press him. "Stan. Can you take his spot?"

"Yes sir." Stan gripped the handrail mounted on the cabin as he moved into position next to Bruce. His legs straddled the stanchion as his feet hung over the edge. His chest was braced against the lifeline. "Ready."

Phil turned to Justin. "Hang in there. Right now it's gotta be ladies first."

"That's if we all don't drown first," Justin said. "Can't you at least untie me?"

"Negative. Don't panic. You're next. I promise," Phil said.

Still treading water, Phil shifted Jodi's limp body so it was suspended between his outstretched arms. He then aligned her body parallel to the boat. He looked Bruce and then Stan in the eyes. "Wait for my signal. Remember, use the tilt of the boat for leverage. Be careful to support her neck."

They nodded.

Bruce glanced over at Stan. "Let's do this right for your brother, Bobby . . ."

An earsplitting bolt of lightning ripped across the sky.

"I was thinking the same thing," Stan shouted back.

"Watch me . . . watch me," Phil commanded.

A sudden volley of waves beat against the boat, pushing the deck upward with a wicked heave. Just as suddenly, the deck dipped toward the surface of the water.

"NOW!" Phil shouted.

Phil kicked and hoisted Jodi up with all of his strength. Bruce and Stan, arms outstretched, struggled to yank her body from the grip of the angry water. Just when they managed to wrestle her onto the edge of the boat, another battery of waves, like the jaws of a pit bull, tried to drag her back into the bay.

"Hold on!" Bruce said, clutching Jodi by the vest.

"We got her . . . we got her!" Stan yelled.

Phil shouted, "Good. Get her inside. Quickly. Bruce—you know the drill. Use the smelling salts . . . in the emergency kit. And stabilize her body temperature."

"Yeah, but what about Justin?" Bruce asked.

"I got him. Now move!"

8:29 A.M.

"Captain, I see the target vessel," said Frank Wells, engineer of the forty-one-foot UTB utility boat, a favorite workhorse used by the Coast Guard Search and Rescue team. With a top speed of twenty-six knots, an aluminum hull with a four-foot draft capable of handling wave heights up to eight feet, and a range of three hundred miles, it had both the speed and the ideal design for most operations in the Chesapeake Bay. Frank Wells, along with the coxswain and two enlisted crewmen, had been dispatched to find the *Dreamweaver*.

"Sir, we have a situation," said Wells after a moment.

"How so?" asked Captain Jeff Bridges, the coxswain in charge of this mission. He had been reviewing the details of his operation: a civilian houseboat with seven students, one possibly armed and dangerous, and one adult male.

"She's sitting beam to the wind and she's rockin' and rollin' really bad. I'd advise against a direct board," Wells said, "unless they can bring their bow to the wind."

"Roger that. Bring us around to the downside of the wind; put us thirty yards from the target. Can you raise them on the radio?"

"Negative. It's reported to be down."

"Cell phone?"

"Negative."

Bridges considered the options. "Once in position, we'll make contact with the loud hailer."

The loud hailer was a high-powered megaphone device permanently mounted on top of the wheelhouse adjacent to the radar and antenna mast. The impressive array of electronics topped off the white boat with its dominate red-and-blue accent stripes. The UTB both looked and moved like the cavalry charging into battle to save the day.

The Guard ripped through the waves. Three minutes later, Wells said, "Sir, we're in position."

The coxswain grabbed the microphone. "This is Captain Jeff Bridges of the U.S. Coast Guard. Please acknowledge."

A long moment passed.

"I repeat. This is Captain Jeff Bridges of the U.S. Coast Guard. Please acknowledge."

Phil stepped out onto the rear deck but maintained a grip on the cabin-mounted rail. He held his megaphone up to his mouth. "Ahoy, captain. Phil Meyer here."

"Mr. Meyer, what is your status?"

"Everything is under control—except the boat itself."

"Can you get the bow to the wind?"

"Anchor is jammed. Working to correct."

"Do you need any kind of assistance?"

"Roger. A medical emergency on land requires . . ."

"Say again."

Phil tapped the side of the megaphone and tried again. Nothing. He threw his hands up in the air.

"Stand by." The coxswain lowered his microphone and turned to his engineer. "What do you see?"

"Batteries must be dead, sir," said Wells, looking through high-powered binoculars.

"Did he say 'medical emergency'?" Bridges asked.

"Roger that."

Bridges shook his head as he watched the houseboat heave and bob in the high winds and waves. If he pulled the UTB alongside her, the two boats would likely collide, damaging and, more likely, sinking both. It was just too risky.

"Wells, this looks like one for the helo ops," Bridges said. "Contact the Air Guard. Give them the coordinates."

"Done."

Bridges raised the microphone. "Mr. Meyer, we cannot board to assist your emergency—not in your present position. We've requested assistance from the Air Guard. Their ETA is twenty minutes. We'll maintain our location until further notice. Over and out."

Jodi and Justin had changed into dry clothes. Both sipped hot chocolate in the main cabin. They and the other students sat on the floor for safety as the houseboat rocked in place. Jodi looked up as Phil entered the room. He held on to the doorjamb to steady himself.

"How do you feel, Jodi?" Phil asked.

"Yeah, you sure looked mostly dead," said Bruce.

"Um, fine . . . ya know, considering everything." Jodi managed a smiled.

Heather reached over and patted Jodi's back. "Glad you made it, girlfriend."

Jodi coughed then cleared her throat. "Me too."

"By the way, Jodi, looks like you're gonna get the miracle you prayed for," Phil said with a broad grin.

Jodi cradled the mug in her hands. The warmth felt good to her touch. "Let me guess, all I have to do is swim out to that Coast Guard boat and ride off into the sunset?" She set the cup down and then crossed her arms. "No way. I . . . I still haven't dried out from the last episode of *Jaws*—thank you very much."

"That's not what I had in mind."

"Well, then . . . like what?"

"Ever been on a helicopter?"

Jodi scrunched her nose, unsure of his meaning.

"Oh, I get it. Are you serious?" Bruce said. He exchanged a knowing glance with Phil. "Cool beans. This'll be like a scene right out of *Rescue 911.*'

"Yeah, but where will they land?" Carlos asked, evidently aware of what Phil had in mind.

Stan said, "They don't land, meathead; they . . ."

"Careful now," said Phil.

"Oh, sorry. They'll lower down a dude in a basket or something, Jodi gets in, and—whoosh—she's outta here," Stan said.

Jodi started to get the picture.

"Time out. You want me to do what?" Jodi ran her fingers through her damp hair.

Phil dropped to one knee. He spoke, using his hands for emphasis. "It's an air-to-sea rescue. It's perfectly safe, Jodi. These guys are professionals. Rescue is their full-time business. And yes, they're your only hope of being transported off of this boat in time to reach Kat. They'll be here in a few minutes—that is, if you still want to help Kat."

Jodi bit her lip. *Boy, this sure brings new meaning to the idea of being a living sacrifice,* she thought.

"Of course I want to help her," Jodi said, twirling the ends of her hair. "But thirty minutes ago I was unconscious. I'm still water-logged . . . I've got scrapes and bruises in places I didn't know existed . . . and now you want me to play Mary Poppins—in that mess?"

At first, no one spoke. The constant whistle of the wind could be heard through the windowpanes as strong gusts whipped the rain into a frenzy.

Vanessa picked at a thread on her life vest. "She's got a point. I mean, like where do you draw the line to help somebody out? She's tried already . . . doesn't that count for something?"

"Me? I wouldn't do it," Carlos said. "No way, José. In fact, I think this whole rescue thing has gone too far." He stuck out his jaw. "Hey, that's just my opinion. But like . . . how much should *we* go through to save one person?"

"Actually, isn't Jodi the one who's giving up the most here?" Heather asked. "I think she's doing the right thing."

Jodi looked intently at Phil. "What can our star Seal tell me about the helicopter um . . . experience?"

"I'm gonna bet they're using a HH-65 Dolphin helicopter. It's a fully loaded, very reliable medium-range craft with a four-man crew," Phil said. "Typically, at least one member of the crew will be a certified EMT."

"Say what?" Stan asked.

"That's emergency medical technician," Bruce said.

"In fact, do you hear that drone? Sounds like they're almost here." Phil rose, walked to the front door, and scanned the cloudy sky. "Yup, that's them—big orange. At least that's what we used to call them. They'll be here in less than a minute and they'll probably hover directly above us at forty to fifty feet." He turned to Jodi. "You'll do fine. Isn't this what you prayed for?"

She swallowed hard. *Was* it what she prayed for? Or was Vanessa right? Maybe trying was all God cared about. Then again, last night she had felt so strongly that God wanted her to be a living donor for Kat. Her eyes searched the faces in the room.

"I . . . I just wish there were another way," Jodi said.

"Would you get a load of this?" Bruce said, his face pressed to the window. He stood by Phil near the front door.

Jodi didn't feel like getting up. "What's happening?"

"That helicopter is *huge* . . . about half the size of our boat.

Right now they're lowering Tarzan down a cable with a wench or something," Bruce said. "How cool is that?!"

Stan and Justin rose to get a look.

Jodi turned to Heather and shrugged. "Must be a guy thing. Me? I'd like to be in bed for a month."

"You do look kinda French fried, Jodi. You okay?" Heather asked.

"I'm all right, I guess." Jodi took a deep breath.

"Hey, flyboy's on the deck. Looks like a SWAT team member in that black wet suit, ya know what I mean?" Stan said.

Jodi looked up just as the front door opened. Phil moved aside as the newly arrived guest stepped in. Jodi noticed he wore a shoulder-mounted microphone like the police used back at home. He removed his yellow-tinted goggles and stood at attention.

"Good morning. I'm Lieutenant Cy Smith with the Coast Guard Air Station in Atlantic City, New Jersey. I'll be your escort today. Could you tell me the nature of the medical emergency?"

"Welcome aboard. I'm Phil Meyer," he said and shook the lieutenant's hand. "One of our students had an accident yesterday damaging both kidneys. She's been transported to the Abington Hospital. Both kidneys have failed and she's in desperate need of additional blood and a donor kidney."

"How do we fit in?" Cy asked.

"The patient has a rare blood type, which Jodi Adams," Phil pointed in her direction, "happens to match. Jodi needs to get to the hospital ASAP. Can you transport her?"

"Stand by." Cy activated his belt-mounted radio transmitter and spoke into his microphone. "Cy to commander."

"Go."

"Lower the basket. Prepare to receive healthy subject for transport to level-one trauma center," Cy said.

"Roger that."

Cy took several steps toward Jodi and gave her his hand to help her stand up. He looked her in the eyes. It was as if he could read the fear she felt. "Forget about what you've seen in the movies, Jodi. You're gonna be just fine. As you'll see, the basket is about two feet wide by three feet long. There's a railing about twelve inches from the bottom." He motioned with his hands as he spoke. "The four metal posts from the four corners which meet at the top are where we connect the cable."

Jodi could see the basket dropping into view on the front deck.

He followed her glance out the window. "Great. You'll notice there's a flotation device mounted on the front and back. I'm going to ask you to keep your hands inside the basket at all times. The whole thing takes less than a minute. We'll be airborne in no time to help your friend." He gave her a reassuring smile. "Questions?"

Jodi tucked her hair behind her right ear. "Just one. Has the cable ever snapped?"

"Never. Are you ready?" Cy asked.

Heather quickly rose and stood by Jodi's side to whisper a short prayer in Jodi's ear. "Jesus, go with Jodi. Keep her safe. Amen."

They embraced for a brief moment. When they released, Jodi looked at Heather and noticed a tear roll down Heather's cheek. "Thanks for praying," Jodi said. She wiped away Heather's tear. "Come see me as soon as you can, okay?"

"Will do."

Jodi turned back to Cy. "I guess I'm as ready as I'll ever be."

Cy held Jodi's arm to steady her as they headed for the front deck. Once outside, although the rain hadn't let up, she felt the wind start to ease for the first time all morning.

She watched Cy reach up and grab the basket, which swayed a few feet above the boat. He nodded to the engineer in the helicopter, and the basket was lowered to the deck. He held Jodi's hand as she stepped inside, sat down, and drew her legs to her chest.

"Remember, keep your hands and legs inside."

"Hey, there's no seat belt?" Jodi said with a nervous laugh.

"Trust me. You won't need one. If it helps, don't look down. You'll do great!" Cy took a step back then spoke into his mike.

With a jolt, Jodi felt her aluminum cage grow wings as the earth disappeared beneath her.

Warm tears mingled with the rain on her face.

Friday,
Abington, Pennsylvania

2:17 P.M.

Jodi Adams lay motionless on a gurney in the recovery room of Abington Memorial Hospital. A soft chorus of mechanical beeps mirroring the cadence of her heartbeat was monitored by the attendant at the nurses' station.

Her mother and father were at her side, proud that Jodi was willing to make such a sacrifice. Mr. and Mrs. Adams had arrived at the hospital soon after receiving the Coast Guard's call, and they took turns staying with Jodi during the three days it took to monitor Jodi.

Rosie rejoined Jodi's parents, having stepped out for lunch and some fresh air during the three-hour procedure it took surgeons to remove Jodi's kidney. According to the latest doctor's report, Jodi's parents informed her, Jodi should regain consciousness in a few minutes. Kat, meanwhile, would require another four hours in surgery to receive the organ transplant.

The ordeal was nearly over for Kat, Rosie thought, and yet, she knew the scar Jodi bore would last a lifetime.

Deep in thought, Rosie looked away from Jodi's sedated body to gaze out the window. She nursed a cup of coffee from Starbucks as she reviewed the rush of events over the last few days. Hindsight, she thought, was always twenty-twenty. So was Jodi right? Had the circumstances and timing leading up to the donation of blood and the kidney been a miracle? Or mere coincidence?

Was God's hand at work as Jodi believed to save Kat's life?

Something else bothered Rosie.

She couldn't help but wonder whether she was at fault for Kat's accident. After all, if she hadn't yelled at Kat just as Kat was about to jump, maybe Kat wouldn't have injured herself. On the other hand, Rosie believed Kat was wrong for choosing to ignore the guidelines. No, this was a consequence of Kat's decision, and Rosie wasn't about to feel guilty about it.

So why did Jodi take it upon herself to bail Kat out? Even as Jodi was being prepped to give blood, she had presented this dilemma to Rosie.

Rosie remembered the conversation.

"Do I really have any moral obligation to Kat beyond giving blood?" Jodi had asked. "Even if that means Kat might die?"

Rosie had had to shake her head. "I don't know—I mean, my first instinct is to say no. If it's true that we're just an accident, a product of evolution—you know, 'survival of the fittest' and all that—then, well I guess you don't have a moral duty."

"Well, then, who's to say Kat's life—or anybody else's for that matter—is valuable and worth saving in the first place?" Jodi had asked.

"I guess you'd have to know the answer to that question," Rosie had said. It was just another way to say, "I don't know," and she knew it was a cop-out.

Jodi's eyes had been swimming by then. "It's one thing for a person to donate his or her organs upon death. But humanly speaking, why should anybody be a living donor?"

THE MIND SIEGE PROJECT

"I definitely don't know the answer to that one," Rosie had said. She'd tried to laugh. "I'll be honest with you. I'm glad I'm not in your position, because I can't think of a single reason why I'd want to be a living donor."

Jodi had closed her eyes, and for a minute Rosie was afraid she'd lost consciousness. But then Jodi had looked up at her again.

"I can think of one reason," Jodi had said. "Because it's an act of love—and you'd be doing it out of love for and obedience to a Higher Being. Do you think that's a good enough reason?"

"I don't know what to tell you, Jodi," Rosie had said. "I just don't know what to say."

It still bugged Rosie that she didn't have good answers.

Even now, she wondered what she would do if she were in Jodi's position.

Behind her, Rosie heard a hushed movement. A rustling of sheets. She turned and faced Jodi.

"Ah, I see the patient has awakened," Mr. Adams said, giving his daughter's hand a quick squeeze.

"Hey, Mom and Dad," Jodi said weakly. "Thanks for being here."

"We wouldn't have missed it for the world," her mom said, stroking Jodi's hair.

Jodi turned her head and saw Mrs. Meyer smiling at her.

"Hey, Mrs. Meyer . . ."

"How do you feel, kiddo?"

"Hmm . . . sore, mostly." Jodi swallowed then asked, "How's Kat doing? She gonna make it?"

"She's still in surgery, but I'm told everything is going as well as can be expected . . . thanks to you."

Jodi managed to shake her head. "Not true. I just did what Jesus wanted me to do . . ."

"That's what I can't figure out, Jodi," Rosie said, unsure whether or not Jodi had heard her. She watched as Jodi floated in and out of consciousness.

Finally, Jodi said, "Um, what do you mean?"

"Well, we can talk about this later . . . but why would God ask you to do something so . . . so hard?"

Jodi considered that for a long minute. "This wasn't hard. Giving *both* kidneys . . . now that would be hard." She smiled then closed her eyes for several seconds. "You want the truth?" Jodi paused. "I don't know why . . . I'm still learning things about Jesus myself."

With that, Jodi drifted into near-unconsciousness.

Rosie put down her coffee cup and reached for her purse. She opened it, withdrew an item, and squeezed it into Jodi's hand. "Here, before I go, I wanted you to have this."

Jodi opened her eyes and raised her arm to see the gift.

"Oh, Mrs. Meyer . . . I can't accept this," Jodi said. She was holding Rosie's Olympic silver medal.

"Don't be silly. You're the one who deserves a medal now."

"I'm . . . I'm touched, really I am," Jodi said, a little more alert than before. "Don't take this wrong . . . but I don't need a medal. The best reward is knowing I did the right thing for God."

Rosie didn't miss the inner spark in Jodi's eyes even through the anesthetic fog. Jodi offered Mrs. Meyer a faint smile, then started to fade once again.

Quite unexpectedly, Rosie's tears began to overwhelm her. She took the medal, returned it to her purse, and took out a tissue. Rosie dabbed at her tears then reached to gently squeeze Jodi's arm.

"I guess I've got a lot to learn about this Jesus too," she said. "A whole lot."

Acknowledgments

Bob DeMoss would like to extend his appreciation to

Tim LaHaye for the privilege of working side-by-side with someone whom I respect and admire, who truly has a heart for God.

Greg Johnson, literary agent extraordinaire, for connecting me with Tim LaHaye. How did you know we were kindred spirits?

Mark Sweeney, Ami McConnell, and my new friends at Word Publishing for your professional guidance and your vision for this new series.

Nancy Rue for scrutinizing the manuscript and offering inestimable insight as if it were her own book, and to her real-life ex–Navy Seal husband, Jim, who demonstrated the patience of a saint at my endless questions.

Captain Bruce Johnson for sharing his firsthand knowledge and years of experience sailing the Chesapeake Bay.

Lieutenant Mike Campbell, U.S. Coast Guard Air Station, Group-AirStation, Atlantic City, New Jersey, and Austin Olmstead, Second Class Petty Officer, U.S. Coast Guard, Rating Boatswain Mate, stationed in Maryland who provided valuable details about rescue procedures by the Air and Coast Guards.

Sharon DeMoss for answering my medical queries. Every family should have someone with a nursing background. I'm glad we have you.

Dr. and Mrs. Robert DeMoss for pouring over the nightly batch of pages and for providing specific assistance with world religions, the myth of tolerance, as well as the much needed encouragement to press on. Thanks, Dad and Mom.

Especially my wife, Leticia DeMoss, for her unflinching support throughout the project—juggling the children, holding down the fort, endless errands, and, in general, freeing up my mind to write. What's more, her editorial input was invaluable. Sweetheart, you're the best.